BRIDGE

BRIDGE

Robert Thomas

American Reader Series, No. 23

BOA Editions, Ltd. ❧ Rochester, NY ❧ 2014

Manufactured in the United States of America

First Edition
14 15 16 17 7 6 5 4 3 2 1

Publications by BOA Editions, Ltd.—a not-for-profit corporation under section 501 (c) (3) of the United States Internal Revenue Code—are made possible with funds from a variety of sources, including public funds from the New York State Council on the Arts, a state agency; the Literature Program of the National Endowment for the Arts; the County of Monroe, NY; the Lannan Foundation for support of the Lannan Translations Selection Series; the Mary S. Mulligan Charitable Trust; the Rochester Area Community Foundation; the Arts & Cultural Council for Greater Rochester; the Steeple-Jack Fund; the Ames-Amzalak Memorial Trust in memory of Henry Ames, Semon Amzalak and Dan Amzalak; and contributions from many individuals nationwide. See Colophon on page 156 for special individual acknowledgments.

Cover Design: Sandy Knight
Interior Design and Composition: Richard Foerster
Manufacturing: McNaughton & Gunn
BOA Logo: Mirko

Library of Congress Cataloging-in-Publication Data

Thomas, Robert, 1951–
[Stories. Selections]
Bridge / by Robert Thomas.— First edition.
pages cm
ISBN 978-1-938160-48-6 (pbk. : alk. paper) — ISBN 978-1-938160-49-3 (ebook)
I. Title.
PS3620.H64B86 2014
811'.6—dc23

2014005050

BOA Editions, Ltd.
250 North Goodman Street, Suite 306
Rochester, NY 14607
www.boaeditions.org
A. Poulin, Jr., Founder (1938–1996)

None stir the second time –
On whom I lay a Yellow Eye –
—Emily Dickinson

A rip-tooth of the sky's acetylene . . .
—Hart Crane

Contents

I

II

III

for Cheryl

I

Picnic

David and I like to go our separate ways for lunch. I usually have a tuna-radish sandwich and eat at my desk. The radishes are my inspiration: I like how they clash with my lipstick, and they taste how I like to think my lipstick looks: incongruous. I like to look incongruous—especially to Fran, the office manager, who could win a prize as Miss Fucking Congruity. She'd never go to a bar and grill that didn't match her shoes.

It was hard for David to ask me to lunch, and I liked that, too. It was Indian summer (San Francisco's *only* summer), a hot day last October; we'd known each other three months. The first time he asked, I couldn't speak: I just nodded. In fact I blushed so hard I might as well have been saying yes I'd marry him, and in one of those Mormon celestial marriages that lasts forever and is sealed in one of their secret temple rooms with all the mirrors.

I toured the Mormon Temple in Oakland once. When it was first built they opened it for a weekend to gentiles or whatever they call the rest of us. There was lots of gold and marble, like a Las Vegas casino. *Total immersion.* I've always wanted to be the cowboy wearing one diamond stud at the blackjack table who goes *all in.* The convert who falls backward into the baptismal water, God's love shooting up her nose.

Maybe it's a bad omen if what first attracts you to someone is that they leave you alone. I could tell that David didn't want to leave me alone, but he would if I pretended I wanted him to, even if he knew I was pretending. He *could* leave me alone. Like me, he has a lot of inner resources. Sometimes it's best to keep your inner resources inner, though. Otherwise you may end up with an oil slick of crude in your backyard. Believe me, I know. But mostly it just meant he read books. Our small talk at work concealed another, unspoken conversation: he'd read *American Pastoral* or *The Corrections* at his desk while I read *Beloved* or *Middlesex* at mine. As the word processors of a small law firm, some days our hands are smeared beyond help with all the time we have on them.

When David and I finally had our picnic of BLTs in Bernini Park, I could barely concentrate because of the pregnant woman lying near us on the grass shielding her eyes from the sun with her mystery while her belly in its black sheath absorbed the heat and rose before me like the most blatant sexual organ I'd ever seen. She was *all in*. I couldn't help staring. I couldn't understand how graphic artists and lawyers and even a beggar and his bobtail cat could walk past and continue their ordinary business without falling prostrate on the ground like worshipers toward Mecca.

Catchy Tunes

It's not just this. Every written word is a suicide note. And a love letter, too. There may be no one to talk to who would get it, but if you write it down maybe someone will get it after you've left the room, or in five hundred years, or maybe someone from Sirius, the Dog Star, will get it.

The composer Karlheinz Stockhausen claimed he was born on Sirius. This was the genius who said the crashing of planes into the World Trade Center was the greatest concert ever held because it was performed with utter commitment, although he later conceded the audience had not been given the option to not attend and that somewhat diminished its perfection.

I heard Stockhausen interviewed at Davies Symphony Hall before the orchestra played one of his works that sounded to me like the voices of the parents in *A Charlie Brown Christmas* if they'd been arguing about real estate. Nothing like last Sunday at the opera when Rodolfo sang *O soave fanciulla*, oh lovely girl, to Mimì and I couldn't bear it—not that no one would ever sing that to me despite my undeniable loveliness, but that it *would* be sung, over and over, to that Hungarian ham who had as much soul as a stuffed cabbage—and I mean ham in terms of her acting, not her size: she was quite svelte for a soprano. I wondered if David might even say something like it to his wife when she got home all lithe and limber after her yoga class, and I took the bus home from the matinee and sat on my sofa and began these notes, since the alternative was to kill someone—most likely, but by no means necessarily, myself.

As I said, I was not impressed by Karlheinz. His daughter Christel was a flautist in the orchestra, and she joined him for the interview and said her father would take her and her brother out on the lawn of their summer house outside Cologne (this was years before he was on the cover of *Sgt. Pepper*) and teach them to read each constellation as notes on a stave and to sing the words of their favorite nursery rhymes to the stars' melody: "The dog ran away in the snow" and "Go get the sleigh in the cellar." It was a game but it was hard: work and play at once. Their father explained to them, "God does not write catchy tunes." You could tell she meant it to be a charming story, but the audience sat in silence.

Suffer the little children.

Albino

I know David will never leave his wife, the agile Janette, never choose my auburn over her blonde. My mother always told me I was auburn so I looked it up: *white*, from the same root as *albino*. How did it come to mean auburn? Probably the way a freak like me came to look like Miss America, Miss *Auburn* America. The fact is: my hair is brown, and David would never say he'd left anyone, anyway. He'd say they were separating, like an egg.

My mother has tried, more than once, to show me how to separate an egg with one hand, but I'm not interested. What does she have to do with her other hand that makes it so imperative that it be free? Hold the telephone, I suppose, and talk to her sister Matilda. "Thank God you never had children," she'd tell Aunt Mattie when Matilda overcooked the meat as she invariably did when we visited. "Thank God no child ever had to depend on you for nourishment." I explain to Mom over the phone that I don't need to save my other hand for anything—I've got Bluetooth.

David is impeccable. He'd never hint that anything that led him to leave anyone had any connection with *our* friendship. He'd certainly never mention my hair, the way it falls like water. Any separation would be clean, as they don't have any children, and for that matter not much money. *Are* David and I even friends? We've known each other for one year. Have we spoken a thousand words? That would be barely three a day, four if you don't count weekends, so it must be more. But of course many days we don't speak at all.

Fran introduced him to me last summer. She said he'd be working with me a few days a week to "help out" in Word Processing. My first thought was she hoped to replace me but wanted to try him out first. I'd been there for five years. I'd been there when Dolores, Fran's predecessor, left to work at Google. I'd been there when Peggy, Dolores' predecessor, left to marry an expert witness. I can't remember if I shook David's hand. You'd think I would—remember, I mean. It's not as if I'm incapable of appropriate behavior. Other than the occasional sarcastic remark, I am what my mother would call a perfect lady. Other than the one time I told the bookkeeper I wasn't interested in hearing her story—told her some people have *real* problems, not *boyfriend* problems—I'm nearly impeccable myself, and that's not sarcasm. It's the simple truth.

Asylum

I grew up on the coast in Pescadero and wanted to be a marine biologist. I thought it would be just me and a pencil in a red bathysphere: intimate, warm. I'd observe squid and sardines, their black clouds and silver wheels, and they'd be amazed by my nimble, note-taking fingers. In fact the last bathysphere must already have been preserved in the Smithsonian by the time I left home for college fifteen years ago. Now they use a two-man vehicle, like Jacques Cousteau's *Denise*.

I'm trying to explain what happened when everything began to go wrong, when I could solve differential equations but could no longer walk from my room to the library because the trees were *growing*.

The redwoods had always been an asylum to me. Now their grace only reminded me of my awkwardness. When I looked at their perfect branches, it felt like the time I walked in on Caitlin, my roommate, one Sunday afternoon while her boyfriend was kissing her breasts, naked and shameless and matter-of-fact as knees, and she looked at me with pity and contempt. It didn't matter if I looked like Cleopatra. She looked like Amy Winehouse.

Even the books in the library were naked, which once had looked so beautiful with their buff and russet bindings stacked like layers of sandstone in a sea cliff, but I was the one who felt shame. I didn't need to work myself into a rubber suit and ride the *Denise* into the pink anemones of a coral reef to feel out of place.

The faucet that jutted from the library's concrete wall was naked, the sequoia's roots simmering in the earth, naked the egg white, naked the yolk, naked the olive and clover, naked the old professor as he lectured on the null hypothesis, naked the young biologist as she measured the kelp forests, naked the seven lost psalms of Jonah, naked the eight beatitudes, naked: the seventy times seven forgivenesses of water, none of them for me.

Ripe

What I want to record here is a "sort of" history, like the ballad of Frankie and Johnny. I can never remember which is which, because they're both boys' names. With *my* name—Alice—there's no confusion. Would it be the same if Frankie were a drummer, his wingtips tapping the pedal of his hi-hat, and Johnny a piano player? It all falls into place if Johnny is a piano player and Frankie a dancer.

I wanted to be a dancer once. At least I wanted to take lessons. My mother wanted me to take violin. She wanted to rule out, right from the start, any chance of my playing a role in any ballad, and I guess you can't blame her for trying to shield me from a pleasure so far beyond her imagination that it looked like pain to her. When I was old enough to move to the city, I went without lunches so I could get ballet tickets, and every ballerina's kick—every *grand battement*—was the rooty-toot-toot of Frankie's forty-four. It might be aimed at my mother or a Macy's clerk who snubbed me, but it was aimed. Last fandango in Frisco.

Most people never go against the grain. If you cut wood against the grain, it splinters, but if you cut meat against the grain, it keeps it tender. They say you reap what you sow, but the truth is most of the time some people are the sowers and others the reapers. I just want to be a reaper for once.

What's hard to believe is that I bought the gun before I'd even met David. It was six months before he got the job at my office and before I stopped seeing Dr. Frost, when she was still encouraging me to make my dreams real. She meant to go to Paris instead of watching a PBS special about the Louvre, or maybe just to treat myself to a steak dinner in North Beach. Dr. Frost failed to anticipate that I would venture into a strange neighborhood to repair the heel on my shoe, be forgotten "while U wait" and told to come back another day, notice a gun shop—something I'd never seen in San Francisco—across the street, and remember Dr. Frost's advice on dreams with such uncanny clarity that I thought she was shouting to make sure I'd hear her over the delivery trucks on Mission Street. I'd been doing "good work" with Dr. Frost, not to be confused with Jesus-style good works. I'd been making progress faster than she would have dreamed possible, if she ever dreamed of me. I was ready to "be the change." I was ripe.

I didn't act rashly, though: I thought it over. I'd learned that much. When I returned the next week, I was thankful the man behind the gun shop counter looked like a movie gangster—black tie on black dress shirt—the humor of it relaxed me. Still, he knew he had something on me. Anyone who walks into a gun shop is a convert. They approach the counter as if walking up a church aisle to accept Jesus as their personal savior, knowing they'll be a different person when they walk out the door: *righteous*. Even the word is a gun's blaze.

I was afraid I'd be rejected as unworthy, as if it were a loan application, but what preacher has refused to lay his beefy hand on a sinner's brow? I might be the first, though, and isn't that the definition of hell: to be the only person there? The one person at the orgy reading a book, one she doesn't even like, *Atlas Shrugged*. I had no reason to doubt.

The black shirt smiled at me and sold me the Lady Smith,
the snub Smith & Wesson I'd chosen long before I went in.
To them belongs the kingdom of heaven. To me.

The Gift

My father gave me a rosewood chess set when I turned twelve. I'd never felt so loved through and through, almost literally, as if I were transparent—and it probably wasn't love, just a lucky, last-minute guess at the toy store, which is probably what most love is, anyway. I took it into my room, shut the door, and determined to master every fork and zugzwang, that position still strangely familiar to me now, where you'd be safe if only you didn't have to make a move.

I'd given myself the perfect gift. When I got the box home, I let it sit on the kitchen table in its wax wrap for hours, safe from the elements, protected from rust. I imagined it at rest in its velvet sack next to its dainty box of bullets. I wouldn't need many. And no sequined wrapping paper could have been more beautiful than the brown sheet the clerk had unrolled and cut along the steel edge in one long, smooth stroke. When I finally slit through the layers to open it, the paper was as delicate and rich as sheets of pastry in baklava, but with a mass of dark chocolate in the center.

I'd never touched one. I loved how perfectly its handle fit my hand: centuries of engineering and design coming together in the "unit," and I knew it would *work*. Unlike toys, religious rituals, erotic techniques, and works of art, I could depend on it. The only other device I owned that fulfilled its function so reliably was my reading glasses, and I used a soft gray cloth just like the one I clean them with to wipe the oil from my fingertips as I dropped the bullets one by one into the somber chambers. I just need to know it's there, like the extra purse I keep hidden in the closet with a money clip and a neatly folded change of clothes.

I don't need a class in safety or marksmanship. If I ever use it, it will be at close range. It may be the only way to get rid of the stranger inside. It may be the only way to get inside someone I love when every other route has been barred.

10½

Number of years I've lived in this apartment: 10½. Number of visitors I've had: 10½. The landlady, of course, Mrs. Gucci. No relation to the fashion designer. As far from a fashion designer as one can get, despite her obsession with her carpets. If I ever do *it*, one of my joys will be choosing a method that leaves a mess on the carpet, not just blood but other, more viscous substances. As far as I know, she's never entered the place after unlocking the door and looking anxiously at my boxes of books when I moved in. I enjoyed speculating on which word in the title *Zen and the Art of Motorcycle Maintenance* made her most antsy.

No Zen was involved in Mrs. Gucci's building maintenance, only her son Michael (short for Michelangelo), my second visitor. Michael found an excuse to visit about once a year, always wearing the same red, white, and blue headband. If the circuit breakers in the building broke or whatever it is they do and the power went out, it was an excuse for Michael to knock on my door and look around, as if he suspected I slept on the couch so I could fill my bedroom with marijuana plants and circuit-busting grow lights.

My parents haven't been here for years, but oh, they were here. They came bearing gifts. They brought me an alarm clock as a housewarming present, actually a nice one I still use, one of those that looks like an old-fashioned radio. I have it tuned to the classical station even though it seems like I'm woken up by one of Vivaldi's fucking *Four*

Seasons almost every morning. They also brought an enormous green salad with about a pound of celery, enough to live on for a week if you were lost in the woods, which I was not. That went down the garbage disposal as soon as they left. Who brings a salad as a gift? It required a visit from Michael to repair the disposal. Celery fibers are tough as fishing line.

My sister and her boyfriend came when they were in the neighborhood once because they'd taken a tour of Alcatraz. I wasn't very hospitable, and my sister wasn't very . . . what's the word? Hospitting? I can't blame her: she'd seen a lot. She'd seen me doing my algebra homework when I was thirteen and we shared a room and the bulb burned out in my desk lamp with the green shade and I unscrewed the bulb to replace it and lifted the lamp to make it easier and when I grasped it, I put my thumb in the socket and the jolt knocked me so hard I fell back in my chair to the floor. Our parents ran into our room from the kitchen where they'd been drying the dishes and I was okay, I was fine, but my sister had seen the pause. She'd seen me pause before grasping the lamp and seen that I'd known what would happen, and in that pause she'd seen how I looked at her. So they had a couple glasses of water because they were hot from their tour and they talked for a few minutes about how the inmates made their cells homey—a whisk broom, a mirror (metal, not glass), shoe polish, a harmonica, dime novels, crayons and paper (as if it was kindergarten)—but then they returned their glasses to the kitchen and left.

I don't know the names of my next two visitors, so I may as well call them Seven and Eight, or maybe Siete and Ocho, the Latino painters Mrs. Gucci sent to paint the place after I'd lived here five years. They did my whole apartment in one day. Siete came early in the morning so I could let him in before I left for work, and even though Mrs. Gucci had picked out a generic off-white, "caffè latte," he painted a swath on the wall and told me if I didn't like it he could use a different color, saffron or wintergreen, and Mrs. Gucci didn't need to know. I told him the white was fine. When I got home at the end of the day, Ocho was there too and they were folding up their tarps but still listening to the mariachi music they'd brought with them and playing it louder than I'd ever dared to play anything. Siete was in charge. I think he was Ocho's uncle, and he probably picked the music. It was kind of waltzy. For a second I thought he was going to ask me to dance, and for a second I thought I'd say yes, but it didn't happen.

Officers Jackson and Zapata might have been the alter egos of Siete and Ocho. There was no doubt I'd remember their names. They escorted me home after picking me up at night on the Bridge, where I'd been standing at the rail looking down at the water. I hadn't climbed over the rail or anything. I wouldn't have been conspicuous if it had been light out. What I'd been thinking was not that I was Jesus when the Devil tempted him to leap from the peak and let the angels save him. No, I was thinking that Jesus was *me*. I was thinking he was just a very unhappy person with no mystery to him at all. Did it occur to me that an angel in the form of a freak whirlwind might catch me before I struck the black water and hurl me like a shooting star across the sky? It did, and though I thought it unlikely, I laughed at myself out loud for a moment so I had a twisted look on my face when the officers stopped their Crown Victoria on the Bridge and asked me if everything was all right. Not just if I was all right, but "everything." I was speechless. Think of everything that goes on in the world, in the universe, or behind the front doors and bedroom doors and closet doors of just one city block. Then ask yourself if everything is all right and try to keep a straight face. Nevertheless, I liked the officers and got into the car without giving them any trouble. Officer Zapata was a woman, and the division of labor seemed to assign her the job of churning out empathy while Officer Jackson drove the car, and I had to admit she did it pretty well, mostly by passing me her French fries and keeping her mouth shut. It also didn't hurt that the back seat was ten times more comfortable than the backstabbing bus seats I was used to. By not trying too hard, I convinced them I was stable enough to go home, but their rules required them to take me there and actually see me into my apartment, to make sure I didn't have an array of drugs or razors on my counter or a scary boyfriend or husband on the couch, and apparently I passed the test.

The half visitor, of course, was David. I'd been afraid he might invite me for dinner with him and Janette, maybe even do something nauseating like ask me to bring a friend, but he didn't and I was grateful for that. He waited until Janette had left town for a weekend yoga retreat or something and I'd mentioned I was going to an opera matinee, and he asked if I'd like to have an early dinner with him after the opera. I said yes. I didn't say, "Sure, that sounds like fun" or anything like that. I just quietly said yes, so he knew and I knew. I had a burger and he had some kind of highfalutin fish and chips, and he drove me home. He drove through the open iron gate to the courtyard of my building, and there was no question of my asking him up or even a kiss in his Corolla. There were only the few seconds when he looked at me and left my insides in a disarray in which the last shall be first and the dead shall be quenched and the elixir shall be mercury and cinnabar, and I did not look away, and he knew and I knew.

Antifreeze

David is proud of his cooking. He tried to impress me once with a story of the carbonara he'd cooked for Janette on Saturday night, tossing burnt bacon and raw egg with his bare hands through hot linguine, that throng of tongues. I could hear them whisper in the kitchen: *Your ear is an oyster that tastes of salt and iodine. I smell the blood beneath your shoulder blades and it is cognac cherry butter on rare steak.*

If only I could go back to that time when David and Janette were happy in their way, which by a strange and inevitable logic was the time when David and I were happy in ours. The change is always gradual when someone first discovers they have power over someone they love and decides to use it. *Decides* is too strong a word. The metamorphosis of love into power has already occurred by the time it's a radar blip.

Is it wrong to desire a pure love, to *be* loved purely? To desire precisely the passive voice of it. The love of a mother for her child is so impure, so dirty, in the gorgeous way a thousand-year-old pond is dirty, its stones slick with the decay of camellias and the once gold skin of koi. The love of the child in return is so different, so pure: the innocence of the egret as it plucks and gulps what it wants from the deep water, its beloved prey nothing but a ripple down a white-feathered throat.

I want a child. I want that pure shot of love, one-hundred-ten-proof mescal, mountain dew, hell hooch, antifreeze.

What infuriates me is that David and his wife have been married for seven years and do not seem to have noticed they have not had a child. They're so busy traveling.

I met Janette only once. She picked David up at our office one Friday because they were going across the Bay to have dinner with David's parents. Janette and I made conversation for a couple minutes while David went to the restroom and combed his hair. She smiled as she told me his mother was roasting a leg of lamb to express her defiant indifference to Janette's dislike of lamb. Janette was the sort of woman who would have known exactly what panties to put on for a promenade on the Kona Coast or an audience with the Pope. Where do people learn these precious life skills? I'm serious: I've never been able to, and I give Janette credit. One could see at once she knew how to carry herself, an interesting, accurate phrase. She walked as if balancing herself like a water jug. She was a fucking *amphora*.

I think that's why David likes me. I carry myself as if I were in front of myself, an awkward bag of groceries with the Skippy jar threatening to burst through because the bag boy let the sack wallow all afternoon in spilled pineapple juice on Lucky's counter. Does anyone over eight or under eighty still drink that swill? They have a choice.

David has a choice. But do I? Does a great white have a choice when it smells blood? No, it devours. No, it is the devouring.

Vissi d'arte

I took the bus home after the opera tonight because I like to ride with the old socialites returning to their Nob Hill penthouses, the only time they ever ride the bus. The "distinguished" man with a scarf that's six feet of white cashmere, the kids in the back with their bling-bling and beer, and me in the middle, heading back to my studio and its Mr. Coffee I've already loaded for the morning, something Tosca would never do. In one month my life has gone from *Bohème* to *Tosca*. In one month I've gone from *soave fanciulla* to *femme fatale*.

As the bus lumbered on, I saw Mirella Freni on Van Ness Avenue being escorted to dinner after the show. Wild salmon had been flown in just for her from the Hebrides, and that was only the appetizer. The table would toast her—*To the Voice!*—while her attention wandered.

Every night she must have to get *out* of character so the role can take her by surprise again. The corny scenery, the candelabra, the fake silver chafing dish in Scarpia's dining room all must cause her to flash back for a second to the priest's house in her own home town of Modena—the priest's maid serving her and her mother *nocino* before Father Moscato placed his hand on her shoulder to hold her back while her mother put on her winter coat—and then she sang everything she had to say to Scarpia, and the audience knew it and it was everything *they* had to say to their husbands and wives and priests and baristas and gods.

At intermission I was in the balcony reading the program, mastering the medieval distinctions between orders of angelic contributors, how many thousands of dollars separated cherubim from seraphim, the city shakers whose martinis already awaited them, olives bulging, at their reserved tables.

I imagined I saw David down the row, shoving past the drag queen seated next to him to come to me. I imagined gathering my coat when he suggested we stroll down the marble stairway and claim as ours a pair of vacant seats in the dress circle for the final act. Our knees would touch all during *E lucevan le stelle*, and we would not move them apart for that brief eternity.

It was only when Tosca discovered her mistake—that Mario's mock execution had been real, no *act*—that I looked up and saw David *was* at the end of the row, sitting with his wife in her hot pink dress, and I considered making the transition from acting to action myself.

As soon as I got home I opened a pint of raspberry sorbet and it was only after I had vomited into the kitchen sink that I remembered where I'd seen that color before. Whoever said love is in the heart knew nothing. It is in the esophagus, it is in the enzymes, it is in the gut's acid, and it is in the liver's bile.

Voices and Weather

It was almost an afterthought to take it to work. I couldn't find my pearl earring—my one pearl earring—and looked in the nightstand and there they were, earring and pistol, and it felt natural to put both into my purse. I didn't intend to use either. Dr. Frost might question that, but I take my driver's license everywhere too, even though I never drive. It's the feeling of power, the turbocharged engine that can go from zero to sixty in three seconds but is only driven to church on Sundays. I love that roaring inside me. I'm a *driver.* I can go *anywhere.* I'm a girl with one pearl earring. I'm a girl with a gun.

Crazy talk works. When a parked car starts rolling down Fillmore Street, you leap in and drive it. When you hear a voice shouting at you like a drill sergeant—*Worm! I will turn you into a minister of death*—sometimes you can ride the voice, get control of it by shouting its lines yourself. You're not possessed; you're *taking possession.* If you listen meekly, it doesn't have to break you: you're already broken. The hurricane didn't flood New Orleans because the storm surge was so high. The city flooded because the levees failed. The waters broke through because the levees were built of sand instead of strong Louisiana clay. The water broke through them long before it rose over them. That's why St. Bernard and Jefferson and Plaquemines Parish are underwater. That's why I am.

The voices are clever. When I heat my Top Ramen on the stove at night and tap a dash of cayenne into the pot and think *Again, tap it again*, how do I know that's not someone else's voice? It's not a simple question. If it *were* someone else's, wouldn't it be easier to tell it no? Don't people who hear voices have *more* independence than people who think the voices they hear are their own? *What an idiot*, they think, when Bush is on TV, or *What a liar* when they see Hillary, without a clue that those voices are not their own. Like couples who come to look like one another as they get older, wearing their matching earth tones and floppy canvas sun hats and the pale complexions they've salved with sunscreen, first you hear a high-pitched voice barking strange noises in a foreign language. Later the voice darkens and becomes intelligible: *Don't touch that*. Finally it's burnished with a rag into a soothing voice that sounds like your own and you barely hear it now. You just don't touch because who would want to.

Every visionary, every prophet from Muhammad to Joan of Arc, transmits the same message: *this is war*. Sometimes it takes a voice to tell us to do terrible things, someone who knows we're at war and terrible things must be done. Go to your film festivals and watch the autumn leaves ignite. Enjoy your liminal dusk light, your midnight sun. Perform your exquisite cinematography. It doesn't matter. It's always noon. The earth may not be at its hottest, but that is when the sun burns you the most intensely: before you've noticed the heat. Those who burn easily know. Those like me who do surveillance behind enemy lines. The enemy being those who think we're at peace. Their birthday parties and relentless candles. Blowing their breath out their mouths, aiming it like snipers.

Sometimes it's dark when I walk home from the bus stop and I watch them: the boy doing homework at the kitchen table while his mother opens cans of tomato sauce. Unaware. The man changing the oil in his car in his incandescent garage. Unaware. *Shelter in place*, I want to tell them. *Take cover.* And they would if I told them to, like dogs told to stay who are found, long after their master has died, sitting on the kilim rug no one has ever prayed on in the hall as the mail piles up through the slot. The power of the voice is easy to dismiss by those who have never heard it. Take cover from *me*.

My only fear as I stood alone at the mirror daubing my lipstick, my only fear as I waited at the microwave for Fran to heat her tom kha gai soup so I could heat my Campbell's, as I read the review of *Brokeback Mountain* and David and I talked about Ang Lee and agreed that Christina Ricci was the best thing about *The Ice Storm*, and as my bus crested the hill and I saw distant lights of fishing boats at the wharf and the flashing cameras of tourists as they emerged from the blue neon of Alioto's Restaurant and the gold of Ghirardelli Square, was that I would hear the voice that would order me to destroy it all.

There are sailors who've spent their careers on submarines waiting to hear the order to launch their Trident missiles, and they ask themselves, as I do, if they would have the courage to disobey, and if they would have the courage to obey. They count themselves lucky if they get to collect their pensions and sip vodka Sea Breezes in their ranch homes in the valley without having heard it.

I was lucky today. I know how easily I could have been locked into the moment I dread, told to take the gun out of my purse and aim at the target—someone I work with, say, someone with a slapdash part in his hair—and squeeze the trigger. But that's not the moment I dread. That moment is when the other voice, the chainsaw, countermands the order and tells me to kill myself—before I hurt someone. And that's not the moment either. The moment is when I hear the soft voice that strangely can be heard over the others as it explains why I must execute the original order after all. The cycle goes on and on, the chainsaw alternating with the silent garrote, seductive as a guitar string.

Yet when the voices are quiet, I miss them. No one wants to live in an eternal noon. Most days, hearing voices is the price I pay for the shade of the clouds they thunder from. But some days are like today. Today there was no Mayan god of rain with iridescent scales. There was no Hindu god of rain on a white, four-tusked elephant. There was no Babylonian, bull-horned god of rain, no Chinese god of rain in the form of a silkworm, no Hawaiian god of rain in the form of a blue marlin. There was no Aztec god of rain whose thunder is a jaguar's roar demanding human sacrifice. Today no gods demanded sacrifice. There was no flood; there was no hurricane. Today there was only the rain.

And Counting

There must be nothing like your first time. Being read. Who would read these notes? Mrs. Gucci, after unlocking the door to see why I haven't paid the rent? It would serve her right for not cleaning the shag since the 1906 quake. Or, of course, a cop. Cops and priests: out of fashion but still the ones called to shrinkwrap the dead.

My "next of kin" and David might be next in line to read my drugstore memoir, but a cop would be first. How could it have the intensity for David—no matter how much he regrets the blackberries he could have picked for me with bleeding hands—as it would for the cop who finds me? Would she take my sheaf of leaves home and rest on it her tumbler of Scotch? Rake me. Pile me. Burn me.

This morning I walked past flower stands on Powell Street, roses from Ecuador bred to be crisp and erect. Not obscene udders like the yellow roses on David's shelf from Janette's garden. Does he *like* her dirt-stained knees? I might as well be on my knees myself, praying as I write this. God's a better reader than listener anyway, and He writes better than He speaks. Song of Songs, the Psalms: "Thou hast smitten all mine enemies upon the cheek bone." You can't make up shit like that.

The point is this: I've got my legs curled up on my comfy couch, and I can even see a corner of the Bay, not the sunset or anything, but its effects—the candy orange building across the lot turning, for an hour, a tawny fawn.

Even the aria coming out of the stereo I bought on Amazon sounds like burnished bronze at this time of day, as if it's emerging from mahogany speakers with lion-claw legs in a Venetian palazzo.

And yet I haven't slept for forty-eight hours and counting. And yet when I look at myself in the mirror I see only clouds, the barred kind that vanish like the moisture on a windshield when the defroster is turned on. Flecks of flecks. What one sees if one can see anything in a wind tunnel.

Bloodstain pattern analysis can verify the velocity of objects that have shed blood. A drop of blood in flight forms a sphere, not a teardrop. The cast-off pattern results from blood thrown from an object in motion, the drip pattern from blood falling on blood, the swipe pattern from the transfer of blood from a moving object onto an unstained surface, its direction determined by the feathered edge.

Conduct an investigation, Officer Zapata. There are clues everywhere. Look at the spice rack. Look at the closet: it runneth over with a shining cascade of mail-order clothes. Look at the books face down on the floor.

Blue Angel

I still have last year's holiday card: *Love, Mom and Dad*. In Dad's hand, of course. From the box he keeps next to his typewriter ribbons and his old Hermes. I'm surprised he doesn't wrap his gifts with those ribbons.

My secular Dad with his faith in equations and quasars. I was tempted to get a crèche just for him: the whole nine yards of alleluia, the kneeling ox and the ass. Tempted to glue a cat's claw to a manger scene and send it down the coast to him. There was still time by FedEx. He'd only have asked if I'd taken my meds and criticized me for wasting money on him. It's enough to make me want to move to New Orleans and carry pig bristles in my pocketbook.

I'm starting to appreciate superstition. The first superstition was a ritual performed by parents to ensure their children would survive them so *someone would be sure to perform their funeral rites*. How perfect. Mom and Dad sacrifice everything for me—so I can devote myself to them even after their death. Bring Mom her Constant Comment, Dad his shoeshine kit with the brush and chamois.

I'll wear a blue clay fish around my neck to ward off the evil eye. Boil an egg in holy water. Wear a red scapular, God's dog tag, so Jesus will know me if I should die before I wake. Rub myself with salt, red pepper, and dirt from a baby's grave. Leave burnt sugar cake and a Ramos fizz in the cellar and shut the door.

Miracles are a fact. A million fish wash up, their carcasses a pink rot and froth of stink on the shore, and one starts to breathe. The one who *wants it the most.* The one who imagines a world where she is not crushed by water. Where color is more than a red glimmer of a predator's throat, touch is more than a tentacle, and taste is more than the venom of the sea wasp that I absorbed at home in the deep, on Ocean Avenue.

What you thought was a wall between you and not-you turned out to be a veil they can part whenever they want. I'm afraid. Most people are afraid. Most people are terrified to change their hair color.

I've seen the Blue Angels. I've seen them go *under* the Golden Gate. I've seen the rocket's red glare. The one F-18 that peels away and goes supersonic. The one who wants it the most. I understand the tattoo of the mermaid on the top gun's muscle. She was the one who climbed out of the water and started to breathe. He talks to her before he pushes the thrust lever: *Hold on, blue angel.*

Once on my way to work on the 19 Polk bus, I sat behind a couple who were drunk at eight in the morning. "She thinks she knows what fucking is," the woman laughed, and I thought she was talking about me. Maybe I'll color my hair blue. Maybe I'll start talking to myself on the 19 Polk: *Hold on, blue angel.*

Liberty Bell

Of course I fell apart. The boss cut corners on my bronze. Skimped on the copper. Listen to me toll: wrong, wrong, wrong.

Ben Franklin put me together again with electricity and string. I'd bite down like a dog on a stick for him. Woof, what a man: not the telephone, not the light bulb. He invented the *post office*. He thought he could have his way with me. Thought I was one of his French dancers because of my curves, but Washington hid me underground after the Battle of Brandywine so the British couldn't melt me down.

By the time I was lifted back into the light, someone had figured out I was just good for show. I'd been recast by a master, my tone so pure it could make sinners repent and saints turn to sin, but it would never be heard.

To be wounded is not the same as to be hurt. Wounds stay open. The un-American ones. The patriotic doctors hate you for your treason, your refusal to heal. They hate it that you have an opening, a crack in the rim. Even their mouths are full of teeth.

How they love their labored symbols: we won't let you *bite your tongue*. It wasn't painful, but it was no breeze—more like a monsoon in a box, the box of *me*, until it blew the *me* out of *memory*. I could have been anyone. A silversmith: Paul Revere. Suddenly I knew everything about candlesticks and soup tureens.

The minister's wife stirred the mutton stew and looked out her kitchen window at the rose-barred, secular clouds overshadowing the church spire and remembered her wedding day, aromas of molasses and mace, citron and sack. She could see just beyond her husband's oak shoulders the world he would never acknowledge. They hate it that you have an opening.

It was years ago that the doctor untaped two silver dollars from my temples—Eisenhower bucks backed by the Liberty Bell and the moon. I didn't miss myself. It wasn't as if I was no one. I was everyone. What I'd thought of as *me* was just a habit. The doctor had no idea what I could see beyond his white coat as he bent over me. The red clouds. The white spire.

The Shooting Party

My first date with David (second, if you count the fish and chips) was not one, of course. He asked me when Janette, the world traveler, was away for a few days. She'd actually gone to Mexico for *Christmas*, leaving him to me because apparently she needed a tan or she'd go crazy. I would have said yes even if he hadn't made it sound innocent. In fact it *was* innocent, if by that you mean that split between body and brain in which David and I are all-too-well matched.

We went to a James Mason retrospective, that movie where Mason plays a British lord who says the Lord's Prayer over a poor guy shot in a hunting accident, a poacher. We'd gone to a matinee to avoid any awkwardness. I don't know what my body would have done if he'd kissed me. It's not just my brain and my body that go in different directions. It's different parts of my body, as if I were an open key ring that no longer can hold together the key to my flat, the key to my mailbox, and the key to the storage room in the garage.

How wide do you open during a kiss? He's not the dentist, but you don't want to bite his tongue. Enough for one tongue to exit as another enters, sliding past one another like disco dancers on a crowded floor. What's that Chinese massage where every spot on your foot is a link to a part of your body? Some men think your mouth is like that. They want to plumb your depths by touching every part of it as if they're playing Battleship, crossing off the squares in your ocean—G7! B13!—until every one of your ships has been torpedoed and sunk and ruby and topaz anemones cover every rusted hatch.

Should I help him undo me? It's *hard* to undress someone. James Mason struggled to unbutton the poacher's shirt to look for signs of life, and there was hardly any blood. The man was as clean as his rabbits. Adrenalin rushes from excitement and fear, flooding the thigh muscles of both hare and hound, but it thickens the small muscles of the hand so it's almost impossible to unfasten a button, fit a key in a lock, or fire a gun. The worst lovers are the ones in love.

Why did Mason pray? He was old when he made *The Shooting Party*, close to death himself, no longer the handsome Hollywood lover. He was weeping for himself when he wept for the poacher, not caring how he looked as his tears fell on the face of the dead man, an old actor himself, grateful for the chance to play one more role.

If David had kissed me I wouldn't have cared how I looked. I might have shot him. Or bitten his tongue. I might have said the Lord's Prayer.

Leverage

What would happen if, as Raskolnikov says, I were to do *that*? Would anyone call 911 when they heard the sound? No one ever calls 911 after just one sound. They wait to hear another. These are people with doctorates in history and engineering: I live in the most educated city in the world. And they wait for a second sound, as if hearing just *one* were not the clearest possible sign. They'd lower the volume for a moment on their Ken Burns documentary, then turn it back up: Count Basie, *April in Paris*.

Would there be readings at my funeral? I'd like everyone to bring something to read, *in silence*, whatever they like—Marcel Proust, *The Joy of Cooking*, and *The Wall Street Journal* rising to heaven in glorious, hushed cacophony. Or everyone could sit in a circle and read one verse from the Bible, *at random*. "They shall spread a cloth of scarlet and cover it with badgers' skins." "Jacob separated the lambs and set the faces of the flock toward the ringstraked." Badgers' skins! Ringstraked! That's what I want to hear.

David would be there, of course, to meet my parents for the first and only time—or would he finagle *another* meeting, perhaps an invitation for coffee and my mother's walnut cookies? I swear I'd rise from the urn, a tornado of ash, if he told them *anything*, whether I liked ketchup on my French fries (gobs), what plants I kept at my desk (pink chaos), my favorite miniseries (*Angels in America*).

I could probably count on David to be tactful. Like a good interrogator or poker player or shrink, he gets more out of other people than he gives, and his smile would disarm even my parents. It disarmed me. Sometimes he can go from Ashley to Rhett and back in half a second. I swear he didn't have those brown eyes the last time I looked. He didn't have that thin brown moustache. He didn't have those ears.

David's mission at Mom and Dad's would be to listen and gather clues: the kitchen cabinet knobs, hand-painted by my sisters and me and still used by our sentimental, frugal parents; the practical books on the shelf (*U.S. Savings Bonds: A Comprehensive Guide*), the absence of fiction; the glass coffee table with the glass bowl of camellias that he would not smash on the brick hearth.

He'd flick the blossoms back and forth across the water, becoming more and more curious how they stayed afloat with their immense burden of petals. Surface tension: one of those simple concepts that becomes more mysterious the more you think about it, a veil of water holding such heavy white whorls.

Leverage. A toddler in nursery school can lift the principal on the seesaw if the fulcrum is far enough off-center. It's how most people get through life. They *leverage* one glass of wine against eight hours of tedium and humiliation, or a few minutes of evening shadows under the cypress in Grant Park against their lover's betrayal, the *tell*, the way he brushed his hair off his forehead as he lied, and the petals float—they don't even get wet.

Naming a Baby

I've had years to think about it. Carl? Carl stuck a pushpin in my back in kindergarten. Laura? The Macy's girl who told me the skirt fit. Michael? Uncle Mike and his clove breath. The pros and cons are always inseparable. Jasmine tea and rhododendrons: the morning at the Japanese tea garden when my mother nibbled her almond cookies and accused Grandma of killing Grandpa with the French fries she'd risen for twenty years to blanch at five in the morning to make up for all the ways she'd failed him.

That's the worst, isn't it? To take the one thing someone does well, the one wildflower that barely survives in the shadow of their mountain of mediocrities, and tell them that's it, *that's* what I hate about you.

The fairy ring of a redwood grove. What gives human beings as much earthshaking pleasure as shades of green? If the Eskimos have a hundred words for snow, we should have a thousand for green. But then there's the history major who wanted to kiss me under the sequoia born while Romans burned Carthage to the ground and Mayans built the temple of El Mirador, and I said no because I had a *boyfriend*.

If only I'd been the kind of girl to grab him by the buckle, how different it would feel to walk now through the Santa Cruz mountains on one of those mornings where the mist is waist-high and nothing apologizes for being alive.

Three-hundred-foot-high branches drink sunlight like a pride of lions drink the blood of a zebra: imperially.

If only it weren't the best reasons to live that fester. If only every salt-bejeweled, oil-bronzed French fry didn't remind me of my *body*.

My grandparents made out on the porch swing for twenty years, a Dixie cup of moonshine in Grandma's hand, and then Grandpa's diabetes gave her twenty years alone, a flask of Christian Brothers in bed with her. And she had her stroke and saw the devil leaning over her with his awful look of compassion. And I was left where no child should be, alone with my mother and father.

To think I once dreamed of having a child . . . I have learned some things. I have learned that human beings don't know what they're doing until it's too late. No, that's melodramatic. I have learned that human beings don't know what they're doing until *after the fact*. And that it's the devil, compassion brimming in his eyes, who says, *It doesn't have to be that way. It can be different, for you.*

And Abraham and Isaac go up the mountain again. And the hills explode with clover and blue lupine.

Bridge

I walked halfway across this morning, and it made me feel ordinary. Everyone who crosses the Golden Gate thinks of jumping. Even the kid with his skateboard pissing off the pedestrians imagines their reaction if he'd careen down the cable from the south tower and launch himself toward Fort Point. It always depends on savoring a reaction you won't be there to witness, not so different from writing a letter like this.

The hedge fund broker thinks of jumping in his velour jog suit. The mother herding her three kids drunk on ice cream. The symphony oboist, the bluegrass picker. The dreamer with her long red scarf, the dreamer in his black Giants jacket . . . but all of them are dreamers.

Better to drink yourself to death with Chartreuse or Benedictine and be found in the morning in tomato vines like an old monk. Better to hang yourself from a beam in the vestry just to have the word *vestry* in your obituary. I might plan my death just to invoke certain words from the dictionary: coloratura, Reykjavík, cast-iron, longitude, salt. That would be a work of art. Not the swan dive from the span, the term itself a cliché: swans don't dive. They flap to earth with extraordinary clumsiness, graceful only in flight. Of course, we're *all* graceful in *flight*. It's not flight that separates the graceful from the clumsy.

The deck is 250 feet above the water: it takes four seconds to hit. We take certain things for granted: gravity, oxygen and, if we're lucky, sleep. We take for granted the joy of being here to register our pain. But pain eliminates precisely the gap between itself and the one who registers it.

What I fear most is that, while one of those four seconds might be exhilarating, in the last long, split second before I hit, I would realize my stupidity: a soldier hiding in a cave years after the war is over. To kill myself only to be mocked at my funeral, over multicolored bean casserole, as if I'd made a *mistake*, like when I was a child in the pageant playing one of the three kings and I'd put on my mother's hat with the green silk grapes instead of my crown because it was the most beautiful thing I knew.

Sometimes I think my whole life has been an attempt to undo that moment, an attempt that has been successful to a disturbing degree. Sometimes I see men, and women too, stop breathing for a moment when they see me because I'm the most beautiful thing they've ever seen—my *features* mean something to them, something real that has nothing to do with me.

What I mean is: I know what Medusa felt like. The snakes of green and white jade intertwined, shining, ecstatic.

Ride of the Valkyrie

It was the summer of the Unabomber. It was the summer of the Ring Cycle.

It's hard to believe that David and I have worked together for only a year. From the first morning, I saw that something was wrong with him. He hid it better than I do, but we recognized each other even if we looked as normal as Tom Hanks and Meg Ryan. He'd learned to pass as one of *them*, and maybe he still didn't recognize himself in the Unabomber.

I'd known the Unabomber would be caught by the FBI, or more likely a cop who pulled him over for a broken taillight, though he wouldn't drive a car. He'd convinced himself that blowing up computer science professors would be heroic as long as he could do it with ingredients he could carry home from the hardware without having to drive. Batteries and nails, matches and rubber bands: American ingenuity. I'll bet he got the parts by mail order, just like I get my T-shirts and skirts. I even order my soap by mail, and he probably did too. He probably walked a quarter mile to his mailbox so the carrier would never see him. This was someone who wouldn't own a *dog*, who lived alone with Douglas firs and their pendulous cones. He wanted to *become* a red cedar.

I don't think Daphne wanted to get away from Apollo. I think she barely noticed him. What she wanted was the heady smell of bay suffusing her skin. She wanted to be as soft and resonant as the wood of a guitar, as watertight as the wood of a canoe. Inject me: I want to be embalmed with volatile oils like an Egyptian queen. Burn me: I want to be the incense that makes God long to crush my leaves into ash on his forehead.

David knows I went to the opera every night for a week, but he doesn't know what that meant—how it altered my chromosomes. It's not about liking the music. I'm not a vampire. I don't drink the blood. It's a *transfusion*. Every night the voices flowed into me. I heard voices in my veins. For me the opera hall is a blood bank, and I take it all in: red and white blood cells, platelets, plasma.

When it was over, I was changed. I was ready. My prayer was answered. I was transformed into a laurel surrounded by a circle of fire. David wandered into it as if he were the River Rhine. As if he could carry me on his current like a canoe, all the way to the North Sea. As if neither one of us was human.

The Bone

Mr. Warnick caught me today as I came in. I only know him from conversations we've had as we picked up our mail from the faux-marble table in the lobby. Mr. Warnick is a retired merchant seaman. They make a lot of money, more than you'd think, and he retired young. He's told me all about himself. Not literally everything, of course, or he wouldn't have anything more to say, and that is not the case.

I listen to him because he seems to want nothing from me, and in my experience that makes him unique. Even Mrs. Oliphant wants something, maybe simply for me to love her dirty white mutt so he'll have someone to turn to when she dies. I wouldn't take him in if he came with a lifetime supply of Milk Bones.

Mr. Warnick is one of those men who love to explain things to women. Do you have five hundred bucks? Mr. Warnick will tell you where to put it: Coca-Cola and Philip Morris. Like cockroaches, Coke will survive Armageddon, and America's neon lights may be eclipsed by the halogen blast of China but four billion Asians will still want to be Humphrey Bogart and smoke.

Mr. Warnick loves America. He doesn't understand people who deny that America is the greatest nation in history. They love France. Someone should tell them: Napoleon slaughtered millions, eighty thousand in the Battle of Borodino alone. In his retreat from Moscow, two hundred thousand *horses* died. Mr. Warnick has seen stowaways from Shanghai emerge from cargo containers where they had lain in their own piss and breathed through a straw for weeks so they could come to Los Angeles.

Don't get him wrong. Mr. Warnick has nothing but admiration for China. He's been to the Lion Grove Garden of Suzhou. He's heard the peals of the Big Bell Temple in Beijing, audible thirty miles away in moonlight. Did you know that China invented not only gunpowder but bells? Mr. Warnick will tell you.

What can one human being give another? Love? Money? *Attention*. God doesn't need love. He wants you to say His name. Like a dog with a bone. That's the *point*. The dog is obsessed *because there's no meat on it*. Man and God: there hasn't been any meat on that bone for quite a while.

Once I brought a file to a lawyer at my office and she asked how my weekend had been, and when I told her about a movie I'd seen, she stopped what she was doing and listened to me *with her whole being*, as if we were alone in the eye of a hurricane, far from the destruction—downed power lines and overturned 18-wheelers—that surrounded us. Then she turned back to her desk. I never forgot it.

Hot Springs

Word processing at a law firm is a curious job. It has a patina of professionalism, less personal than being a secretary, if by "personal" you mean finagling lunch reservations for an attorney at the newest bistro where the chocolate ice cream is made with *fleur de sel*. Granted, the profession is becoming as obsolete as soda jerks and scribes, as attorneys do more and more of their own "input," but we're still useful in a legal Code Blue. We're like paramedics, somewhere between an emergency room resident and a taxi driver. Sometimes the pressure is intense—*follow that car, Jake!*—but there are hours with nothing to do but polish your chrome. It takes a particular temperament, and it suits me. I thought it did until David was hired as my co-processor. And I recommended him! I *wanted* him.

When you share an office with another person, it doesn't matter how palatial it is. Inevitably your sleeve touches theirs when you both reach for a fresh ream of creamy paper. It's more intense than any marriage. David and I sit in a room together, a room that's not very large, just the two of us, *forty hours a week*, with (it's no secret) little work to do. No television. No dishes to wash. No dogs to walk. No distractions. I spent one hour a week seeing Dr. Frost and it was supposed to change my life. Most married couples probably spend forty *minutes* a week together without distractions, and that's on their honeymoon.

Imagine sitting in a hot springs in the mountains with someone for forty hours a week with no distractions but a light snowfall on the fir trees. After a couple weeks you'd want to kill them. Unless they were the rare person who knows how to cherish your privacy *and* ravish it. Then you'd fall in love.

Think of a prisoner in solitary confinement, his only companion a beetle with a yellow band on her back who comes and goes through a crack in the concrete. Every morning the beetle faithfully returns and scurries across the floor while the man talks to her, gives her crumbs from his crust, imagining an echo of the sun's warmth rising from her carapace when he bends his cheek to her. Yes, I say *him* and *her*, but I suspect I am the prisoner and David is the beetle. He is the one who is free, while I wait for him every morning and long for him every night. Where does he go? I imagine him staggering on six spindly legs under streetlamps and throbbing neon stars. I *need* to believe he wanders, but his quest may end in a crevice inches into the wall where he lies all night and listens to *my* heartbeat, his tiny, tender antennae rising in response to *me*.

The prisoner can face any interrogation as long as she can look forward to seeing her ally the next morning, and he knows this, knows how deep the prisoner's love for him is, and still he fears she thinks of him as . . . an *insect*. He doesn't know: his yellow band is all the mystery of the world to her: egg yolks and autumn leaves, pigment from the urine of cows fed on marigolds and mango leaves by the banks of the Ganges, the gold scarab worn by Queen Nefertiti in the tomb. I'd do anything for David. I'd preserve his brittle, little proofreading soul in my rich, resinous amber. How is it we can see into another's soul and guess, with only rare mistakes, secrets he may not know himself, everything about him except the one thing we long to know: how he will respond if we touch him?

¿Qué Pasó?

I was in Monterey once in a Spanish class, and a bomb went off in the street below and not one of us knew how to ask, *What happened?* Happen: things happen so rarely we don't foresee we might ever need a word for it. We barely need verbs at all. Today I needed a slew.

David and I were having our regular Monday morning chat about our weekend. I'm always tempted to shock him by saying I went spearfishing or out drinking in the Mission on Friday night and woke up in the Louvre on Sunday morning, or even went to *church*, which would shock him even more and give me a stained-glass aura in his eyes that would make him whimper when he went to bed with Janette in her transparent glory.

In fact I'd gone to the symphony, and a spotlight had exploded at the climax of *La mer* and I'd been saving that to talk about, when David said—as matter-of-factly as if he'd gone to Wendy's for a Hot 'N Juicy—that he'd moved into a hotel on Market because he and Janette had separated. Yes, after all this time, that was how he put it: not that he and Janette had separated and so he'd moved out, but as if the primary information were his discovery of a charming, bargain-priced pension—he actually called it a *pension*—and the breakup of his marriage deserved only a subordinate clause.

Nothing is as infuriating as someone who acts as if they're just saying something and not *doing* something by saying it. I was prepared for an explosion and there was none. I was prepared for lightning to enter my left shoulder and exit my right thigh. I wasn't prepared for this glacial tsunami.

David's marriage has been a thirty-foot levee between him and me that can't be breached. Never mind how often I've dreamed of it: he's never hinted at any real friction between them over so much as a dinner menu. They both *love* Caesar salad. I should have known: everyone in San Francisco loves Caesar salad. Does he think this is a movie where cymbals crash as Jimmy Stewart kisses Kim Novak and she melts in her stiff gray suit? It doesn't work like that.

No, this was the movie where the tobacco planter sees his whole life pass through his mind as he falls from the gallows, except that I saw my whole *future*: David would invite me out to dinner at an Italian restaurant where the waiter grates lemon zest instead of Parmesan on your fettuccine, and then *in* for dinner at the apartment he'd found where he'd broil salmon with those ridiculous "baby" potatoes. How does any relationship survive baby potatoes?

During one of those dinners, somewhere between the balsamic vinegar and wild mushroom risotto, we'd have The Conversation. "There's something I need to talk to you about. I have weapons of intimate destruction. . . ." No. "I have an illness. I've hurt people. I've hurt myself. I've been in the hospital. . . ."

Somehow we would get through that and he would kiss me, which is to say we would speak in tongues and discover the original word for fire, the word first uttered when lightning ignited a treetop, and the more important word, the second word for fire, when a human first saw *I can make this with my hands and a rock but first I have to split the rock,* and the third, the most important, the forgotten word, when the human saw *I can quench the fire with water, water is another kind of fire, it flows down and cold not up and hot like the other but it flows,* and the two fires, the hot fire and the cold, would flow through us in a thousand lost languages.

I saw all that in an instant and then I saw the creature inside of me, the *mammal,* growing until it committed the original sin, tearing me like meat, rending me to free herself (the *it* now *she*) from my love, and saw—not that it would be a punishment, not God's punishment, although I'd deserve it if it was—but saw that one day she would unnaturally but logically and inevitably *hurt herself* and I must not let that happen, I had the *power* to not let that happen.

Therefore, it doesn't work like that. It works like this. Century-old trees are uprooted like saplings. A piano is crushed like a black pack of cigarettes. People are crushed. People are lost in every way they can be lost. *Separated* in every way they can be separated. He from she. She from it. I from me. My cry was ground into the dirt of a thousand strangers' voices inside me. When silence is separated from sound: no more music, no more *La mer.* When wind is separated from weather: no rain. When prayer. When oxygen. When baby baby baby. Paint rusts. Music rusts. And that was my brave new world, one hundred feet under *la mer.* It wasn't that I couldn't breathe. I could breathe all too well, and one by one the symptoms of excessive oxygen overcame me: disorientation, preseizure aura, and what medical books accurately term prolonged dazzle.

Cause and Effect

Once I had a book with a sketch of a soldier with a hole in his gut where a bullet had gone through him during the War of 1812, and he was smiling, "better than ever." A doctor peered into this keyhole to study him, and that was the origin of the science of modern anatomy. It seems a fable to sell a children's book, but maybe it's true. This morning it seemed as if it could be, as I tucked my blouse into my slacks as if nothing were wrong and I just had to cover the gaping hole. People talk about feeling empty, but this is different. I'm a sail, I'm a fucking spinnaker, and the wind could take me anywhere. I could do anything.

The concept of cause-and-effect is ridiculous. Breaking the link between cause and effect is what it means to be human. Cause: A man gives a woman a spray of pink carnations with serrated edges. Effect: The woman cuts her thumb with a bread knife.

Cause: A woman at a bus stop witnesses a bicyclist swerve to avoid an opening car door and get hit by a bus. Effect: The woman listens to her old recording of Berlioz' *Summer Nights* and is moved by it for the first time.

Cause: A fire breaks out in the galley at Amundsen South Pole Station on Antarctica's high plateau and can't be extinguished. Effect: The woman paints her nails ice blue.

Cause: I see a sailboat disappear behind Angel Island as my bus crests Russian Hill. Effect: David leaves his wife. Cause: I heat a can of minestrone for dinner and garnish it with parsley. Effect: David leaves his wife. Cause: David leaves his wife. Effect: Aretha Franklin becomes the first woman inducted into the Rock and Roll Hall of Fame. Cause: David leaves his wife: Effect: The Leonid meteor showers commence.

Cause: What is the sound of one hand clapping? Effect: The world is *full* of people clapping with one hand. The question is why it is so rare to find someone who knows it requires two.

Cause: Truth is a spectrum of gray, gravel in a Zen garden. Effect: Truth is the colors of a rainforest flower never seen by human eyes, colors that only could be seen by eyes evolved in another solar system, in response to its *other* light.

Cause: Hickory dickory dock. Effect: Sadness that the bidirectional dimensions of space are asymmetrical with the unidirectional dimension of time. Cause: The manifold of spacetime. Effect: The past does not end any more than Chicago ends when you take the train to New York.

Cause: Am I animal, vegetable, or mineral? Effect: Not this, not this, not this.

Annie Hall

I don't see what's so bad about it myself: the Iraq War. Every once in a while I've given David a glimpse of how conservative I am—*in some ways*—and I could tell it excited him, as if I'd left a button undone on my glam rock blouse.

Last month Fran warned David and me the firm had a trial coming up and she hoped we were "up to it." She was very casual and la-dee-da about it. Fran is very Annie Hall about almost everything, even Iraq. Fran likes vests. Everyone says it's an androgynous look, but Fran's about as androgynous as Betty Boop. I'd never wear a vest. I'd never feel up to it. At least with the trial I knew David and I would have something to do besides discuss the news, although it still gives me satisfaction to flick my newspaper into the trash every day while he recycles his. Where does he think it *goes*?

It goes into an inferno where the ashes are glued back together in the parody of paper used in greeting cards sent to all the hopeless, fucked-up people in the world to cheer them up. I'm *not* up to it. It's all I can do to recycle myself every morning. I'm the blue and amber shards the glassblower melts and rolls like honey to form a pale green decanter so a man can pour iced tea into a glass on a terrace on an ordinary afternoon.

What I would give for that afternoon: how many people would give anything for an ordinary afternoon, a shaded table, a carafe of tea. . . . Some people live their whole lives without ever wearing a simple sun hat with a yellow brim. *I've* never worn a hat with a yellow brim, or eaten a poached egg in a bistro, or grown a tea rose in a garden, things people have done for centuries, yet how impossible they seem, what an accomplishment.

Millions of years of evolution so a woman can sit in a café wearing a sun hat and reading a book. Maybe she's breaking up with her boyfriend, like Annie Hall, and it's all right because she has a small pitcher of rose petal tea in the shade. What would a hostage in Karachi give to sit in a café and sip tea even if his girlfriend or wife or *mother* had broken up with him? The breakup would be no more than a dust mote in his eye. Shouldn't we do *anything* to free him?

It's not about oil in Iraq: it's about tea in Islamabad. Not about how much blood has been shed but *how absolutely it has been worth it* so a woman can read a book, by herself, in a café—free to leave her home, free to be out in the street.

Your Majesty

The worst is to be understood, as if you're nothing but a retro bellhop who delivered a telegram and is free now to skim a girlie rag or listen to the Yankees game or, well, *die*. Mission accomplished. Message understood. Crumple it. Suck it. Swallow it. I've always been more like the post-modern bellhop in *North by Northwest*, paging someone who doesn't exist (but is a Cary Grant lookalike) to deliver a message that doesn't exist. But that all may be about to change.

I wonder if Cary Grant ever felt like a bellhop. I'll bet George W. Bush has felt like one all his life. I'll bet Princess Diana felt like one. "May I get you a spot of tea, Your Majesty?" Her *Majesty*: what does that even mean? French horns have majesty but not violins, Bach's organ but not Chopin's piano. Christians love the organ because in Rome it was the background music when lions martyred them in the Colosseum. It's like the sun: beauty without tenderness.

The majestic, horrible thing is that David understands me. When Dr. Frost told me it was all right to keep secrets from her, I expected a bevy of Valkyries from the American Psychiatric Association to strike her with lightning. People always think they understand. They hear the voice of *God* and think it's saying . . . *What* do they think it's saying? "Thou shalt not kill." Right. God, the inventor of death, said *that*. To God it's all a movie, like the blood in *The Wild Bunch*: corn syrup and grenadine. "No animals were harmed in the making of this movie" does not apply to God. He was grandfathered in when they made that rule.

People always think they've "got your number" and deserve a Nobel Prize when they've figured out the tritest, pop-song truth about you: you're lonely, you want love, etc. I wish I knew my number. Is there such a thing as an irrational prime? Yes: I'm living proof.

The truth is that anything can add up to anything. A hunter can shoot a deer because he remembers how beautiful his mother looked on the porch holding the tools while his father installed storm windows. A woman can pour herself a glass of wine because the earth turns enough that the sun falls on the callas on the kitchen table. A woman can take a man's hand and put it on her breast because she despises him and the street he lives on and the way the moonlight pools in the fenders of the parked cars.

I can turn the page of an old library book because I want to murder the man in the hardware store who sold me a flashlight. I'd do it in his sleep so he wouldn't feel a thing. I stay awake at night thinking of all the things I could do to people in their sleep. I can go for a morning swim because I want my skin to reek of chlorine, to smell as if I could bleach a glacier, when I walk past David as if nothing has happened. Something *has* happened. This morning the whole sky wore its bloody lining inside out. David is the stalker who knows whatever you do, it means you love him. The fact that he may be right does not make his conduct any less culpable, or any less cruel. Just the opposite.

Killing myself would be sending a telegram to David in a code only he could decipher. Only he would have the decryption key, and it's such a simple one, the oldest one there is: music. Music. He'd analyze the trajectory of the bullet, the equation of its brief parabola, and translate it to a musical phrase (E-flat, F, D-flat, A-flat). Only he would hear the tenderness in its majestic dissonance. It would almost be worth it just for that.

The Lion's Head

Here I am again on my garage sale sofa the color of one of those overpriced, trendy ice creams, plum jasmine, osso buco sorbet. I paid extra to have the guy deliver the sofa and carry it up the stairs, even though normally I'd rather walk down the street naked than have someone in my apartment see the leftover Thai takeout on my counter and the books on my shelf—see I *have* books on my shelf. Dr. Frost said I was paranoid, but someone who sees the *things* in your *home*—it's as if they're scraping layers of paint off the inside of your skull and revealing the old wallpaper underneath: all the tiny, sentimental roses.

Yet I've come to like my headquarters here in the evenings, looking out at the building across the piazza—all right, across the parking lot—imagining the lives inside, but it's no *Rear Window*. I've never seen as much as a blasé cat in those windows, at most an oblong shape that might be a refrigerator in the shadows.

What do I expect to see? In my experience most people don't *act out*, as my doctor said, very often. Once I was walking down Judah after dark to get some vanilla wafers at the Korean grocery and caught a glimpse of a woman in a tan sweater in her living room at the moment a man touched her breast as she reached to turn off the lamp. Somehow I knew it was the first time he'd touched her that way. If it had happened before, they would have had an understanding. They would have already shut the blinds. It was probably the most erotic thing I've ever seen, and I've seen more than you'd think, *especially* in the hospital. The sound of a paper hospital gown being torn slowly in the dark is not something you forget.

People don't *act* very often, so I remember that scene. People don't make *scenes* anymore. That seems to have been a pursuit our parents' generation exhausted, like swing music. My grandmother stood and walked out of a restaurant mid-dinner, leaving her short ribs to sulk in their "Polynesian" glaze, and took a cab home because my grandfather had called her sister a bimbo while we kids watched and knew everyone else was watching too.

People don't do that anymore. It's the great accomplishment of our generation. Our parents defeated Hitler. We stopped making scenes.

What happened to words? Civilization depends upon people learning to say "I spit on you" instead of spitting. Well, I spit on you, David and Fran and Dr. Frost and the sofa guy. With all the force of a civilization that goes back six thousand years, with all the force of the limestone of the Sphinx of Giza, the lion-limbed king who still keeps his secrets on the west bank of the Nile, I spit on you.

The lion and I: we keep our own counsel. How many years did it take to haul the hundred-ton stones into place in the desert? Making a scene. The head is disproportionately small—they say that six thousand years ago it had the head of a lion but a pharaoh hacked it away to replace it with his own likeness.

Imagine the original lion.

Cold War

Every Tuesday at noon sirens warble as San Francisco tests its emergency alarm in case Putin releases a pack of ICBMs across Alaska while he and W talk peace in Slovakia by a stone fireplace big enough to roast a bear. I saw a photo in the *Times*, both of them laughing in deep leather chairs. It would have been the perfect moment to launch a first strike.

David and I communicate in code now, our own personal CIA. How could I talk to him after his "separation"? He'd want to see another British film with me, and this one would be no matinee. And I'd want him to have sex with me in the stairwell so I wouldn't have to let him into my apartment. I could go in alone and flop on the couch and wait until I had our baby. That *is* what I want with all my fist-sized heart, but even I who can calmly consider killing almost innocent people could not do that to someone—give birth to some Don or, yes, Donna who one day would look at herself in the mirror and realize she was like . . . me. And so I stopped talking to David.

In summer, when we were still speaking, David recommended Proust. Now it's almost winter, and at noon today I took *Swann's Way* out of my purse and set it down next to my Whopper and read it while I ate. David didn't say a word, but it was an unmistakable diplomatic initiative in our cold war.

I read that Nixon's initial overture to China was through his ambassador to Poland at a Warsaw fashion show. I wonder what models wear at fashion shows in Warsaw. Something out of James Bond, I suppose. People are hard on Nixon, but he must have known from a young age that he could never be Sean Connery—or Kennedy. Sometimes I wish I had an ambassador I could send in my place to the office, where I feel as out of place as a fashion model in Warsaw.

David acts as if everything is normal even though he surprised me last night coming out of the café at the corner of Battery and the Boulevard des Italiens after I'd had a midnight cup of chocolate, and he had his coachman drive us in his victoria as cattleyas trembled on my swansdown collar and his horse trotted along the Embarcadero.

Wasn't there a time when it was easy and David and I could share an order of steak fries and laugh about Sting? Once we talked about flying: he said the only time he feels afraid is when the plane descends through clouds and you can just see whiteness, one wing jutting into whiteness. Suddenly it seemed as if he was talking about white orchids and fucking so we didn't say anything more for a while.

Deniability is the key. Nixon needed it when he made his move toward China over a tray of kielbasa and pickled carrots, and I needed it today. David must have thought the siren was meant for him when I opened the book and Swann adjusted Odette's orchid in their carriage and brushed the pollen from her velvet gown.

Red Planet

I'm the funambulist of the Financial District. My abyss is the two-mile "commute" between my apartment on Bay and my office on Battery. Once a man on the bus offered me a drink. He tore his newspaper into strips, raised his can, wrapped one strip around it as if to conceal what he was drinking from the driver, and offered me a sip of his Bud. I shook my head and turned away, feeling I'd been made a fool of. I should have said *something*. "Sorry, I only drink champagne," or "At least you could have wrapped it in the *Times*."

The doctor says I overreact, but do I? I know she means well, Dr. Frost (she bites!), but what does she know? She would point out that even though I haven't seen her for over a year, I still talk of her in the present tense: I guess she did get under my skin, more or less the way one slips a pat of butter and sliver of garlic under the skin of a roasting chicken.

The worst torture is one that leaves no mark. *Everyone* thinks you're overreacting. Everyone thinks your deck was cut by a con man. When someone *renders* your soul, heating it to the point that it separates from your body like clarified butter . . . Well, we're all clarified now, aren't we?

When someone *erases* your soul—and when someone steals your parking space, leaving you in tears behind the steering wheel, isn't that exactly what it is? Soul is the lightning you don't see but know exists because you hear the thunder. The ice you know is buried in the rocks of the red planet because you've seen the Viking photos of the ancient river valleys. The blue note plucked on the double bass so low the audience doesn't hear it and thinks their chill comes from the horn alone.

The last time I saw Dr. Frost, she asked what I wanted, and I had to think about it for a few minutes before I answered, as if I'd paused in the middle of a highwire. *To save my soul.* How afraid Little Red Riding Hood must have been, walking through the woods, only to find the horror where it usually is: at home, in bed, under the covers.

The Goldilocks Zone

There's always a warning. Hours before the earthquake, squirrels chitter and leap from spruce to pine. When the sunset looks like a cannon fired at the sailor's breast, the morning will bring a storm.

This afternoon Fran called me into her office "to chat." Fran may not know me well, but she knows I don't chat. I can't chat any more than I can land a 747 in Candlestick Park. It was all: Me Fran, you Alice. I chat, you sit. She told me about her vacation to Zurich and the Wiener schnitzel she and her husband enjoyed overlooking Lake Zurich. She bragged that she and Dennis had come home in time for his rugby tournament. When I reflect that Fran and Dennis may be the two persons I know most likely to have what is called "good sex," I wonder if it may be as overrated as Baked Alaska.

Fran finally got to the point and asked me how "it" was "going." For a moment I thought she was asking about an impossible pregnancy that somehow she had become aware of before I did. Then I realized she was asking about the word processing "department"—i.e., David and me. Her tone was cordial, like Robert Duvall in *The Godfather*, but it seemed to suggest a horse's head might have been discovered in the LaserJet, blood gumming up the works.

I told her everything was fine, as if I thought she was asking if I had any complaints, as if I hadn't understood that *she* was complaining about *me*. My "performance review"—like I'm first violin in the symphony—isn't for six months so I knew something was up. I hoped I could put her off if I stuck to my story that we in the "department" were still cozily within the Goldilocks zone.

I learned about the Goldilocks zone in Marine Biology. There's more to it than you think. The conditions are so precarious that allow one to go on living, as I know better than almost anyone. A planet must be just far enough from its sun that its waters neither boil nor freeze. A star itself must be far enough from the center of its galaxy that its planets have a metallic, magnetic core to ward off stellar wind, to turn the wind's lethal force into harmless northern lights. I know all about stellar wind.

What would I do if I lost my job? Cut paper dolls out of junk mail? No, I'd end up back in the hospital. I'd end up with the haircut they give you there. There's nothing worse, and I mean that literally. To have people who care about you visit so they can look at you and go home glorying in their own natural, radiant curls.

As it turned out, Fran bought my story, but not for the price I wanted. She said there had been comments about friction in the department and she asked me to let her know if there was anything she could do. I knew it was a threat, but I thought I could manage it. I thanked her and left her office before she could go on. I didn't mention that friction, too, has a Goldilocks zone, that razor-thin range that keeps a spacecraft from crashing when it returns to earth but does not burn through the heat shield the astronauts depend on—that zone where I live.

The Wall

Anything can be justified, but murder is as easy as pecan pie: just pour the molasses and bake it. The so-called preciousness of life. Ice cream is good but even Tahitian vanilla is not enough to render life sacred. Of course the claim is that love renders it sacred, but is it possible for lovers to look into each other's eyes without thinking *This is the part where we look into each other's eyes*?

When I lay on the beach at St. John, half asleep under a blue umbrella, I noticed a man near me extracting pleasure like a bee from every blossoming inch of me, his eyes moving slowly up my calf, never leaping from flower to flower but submitting to the step-by-step order: x, y, z. Stem, pedicel, calyx. Ankle, calf, knee.

When I went to New York last fall, I saw Monet's waterlilies and wanted to drown in them. It would have been like drowning in *me*. I walked *into* them, examining the layers of blue and red and green and black and yellow. When the canvases were discovered after the Second World War in Monet's studio, they'd been damaged, and perhaps enhanced, by slivers of glass fallen from skylights when the town was bombed, and now embedded in the paint. Later, when I visited the Vietnam Wall to see what people saw in it, it was the same: names on the black granite, lilies on the black pond.

Does Fran deserve to live? What does that even mean? Do mushrooms, *fungi*, deserve to live? What is unique deserves to be spared from extinction. The life of a golden chanterelle would be sacred if it were the last chanterelle. At least that's the argument: human life is sacred because, unlike a mushroom, each person is unique.

Maybe Monet was unique, but Fran is not the last member of the endangered species of Fran. There is nothing of the infinite in Fran's love for her rugby fullback. She has never been as excited as I was under the blue umbrella at St. John and in the gallery trying not to set off the alarm while I got close enough to look into the paint and saw something in the pond among the lilies no one else had ever seen: the names of the dead.

New York

Some people make up a fake identity when they travel. I'd never have the nerve, but I understand it. When a passenger in the window seat starts a conversation with a stranger on the aisle, they know it's an act of aggression, and we victims have the right to defend ourselves: I've just returned from New Zealand, I'm an anthropologist, I've been studying the Maori, and I knew I'd won their trust when they tattooed my back with a red fern. Or: I'm in advertising. Burger King? Have it your way? I came up with that.

That's why people travel: to change identities. When Mr. Warnick sees me in the lobby of my apartment building, I might as well be wearing a drenched white T-shirt over my soul. But in New York I blazed an anonymous trail each time I walked down the hall of the Waldorf-Astoria to the ice machine.

Yes, I stayed at the Waldorf, like Marilyn Monroe and Herbert Hoover. When I walked on Park Avenue I could have been a curator at the Met. I could have been a call girl with a specialty in crèche fetishes or a pastry chef deciding how to decorate my croquembouche. I knew I'd have to return, but for seven days I almost forgot, remembering only when I saw an airplane overhead, the memory of San Francisco as vague as a vapor trail.

The sense of freedom started the moment I arrived at JFK and got into the taxi—the cigar smell in the back seat was the most delicious aroma I'd ever known, the yellow paint on the door was deeper than the yellow of any Van Gogh sunflower, and the driver's horn blared as if he'd defend me to the death like a Bernese mountain dog.

When I got to my hotel room, there were no wall plaques but I imagined the history that might have occurred at the antique desk: General MacArthur writing his memoirs, a novelist composing her spare, acerbic sentences, an ambassador penning a world-weary letter of resignation.

New York was a place where rich people *lived* in hotel rooms: nothing was more romantic than that. Being there was being in love without any of the jealousy or pain. Yes, I who am often terrified to walk from my bus stop home at rush hour strolled at dusk in Central Park without fear, beneath the chestnut- and chocolate- and rust-colored elms on the mall. And yes, the thought of walking with David under the elms, our steps hushed on fallen leaves, crossed my mind although this was weeks before he'd even asked me out for lunch.

Fall in New England acts as if it has something to prove, but in New York it's dignified, civilized, a grizzled merchant who's made a fortune from nothing but his understated good taste, who's been in a few scrapes and knows how to handle himself. I was in love. The leaves were reflected in the lake; their trembling in the breeze was multiplied a thousandfold by the rippling water until it was inside me and I was gold and trembling all over.

Baby's Breath

I've thought of starting over somewhere else, like they do in the movies, just to get away from Fran—from Fran and David and Mom and Dad and Karlheinz Stockhausen and the whole *Run Silent, Run Deep* crew, with David as Clark Gable, of course. My chances are as good as Bonnie and Clyde's. Catch a Greyhound bus to Butte. Get a job at the five-and-dime. I bet they still have one in Butte, one with an aisle for notions, whatever they are. Bobbins and thimbles? I wouldn't know a gusset from a gore.

Grandma had a thimble from France she'd let me play with. I'd go up the stairs to the landing, put the thimble on my index finger, and tap it on an upside-down pie tin as I looked out the window and pretended I was in the Resistance, transmitting code to a submarine.

The point is: I tried. I tried to figure out a way to make a nonviolent getaway, but bird-into-bay-window style I kept smacking into the fact that I'd need a job, and in order to get one I'd need a reference and I'd need one from Fran, and once she knew where I'd gone, all of Northern California would know (everyone "north of the Tehachapis," as Mom would say), so I wouldn't be starting over at all.

When Mom moved to California from Illinois, she drove cross-country in winter and fancied herself a sort of pioneer on a wagon train, or one of the survivors of the Donner Party, one who, given a choice between being the eater and the eaten, knew what side her bread was buttered on. The answer to that question is one of many that has never been as clear to me as it was to my mother. In any case, she took a southern route and never ran into any snow at all until the final stretch when she drove up from Riverside and hit a few flurries in the Tehachapis.

The thing is: my mother really *had* started over, not only started over but gotten *her* mother to follow her. It was as if I moved to Butte with my one suitcase, worked my way up at the five-and-dime until I owned it and had turned it into a chain, and hired David and Fran as assistant managers. It reflected a force of will you couldn't understand unless you'd grown up with my mother. She might not have been able to raise the dead, but she could get my father not only to go to church on Sundays but to wear a white rosebud in his lapel as if, well, his daughter were getting married. Every Sunday since I was five had been a rehearsal for my wedding. She'd even planned the cake: apricot filling, baby's breath.

The worst is that nothing would give me more joy than exactly what Mom planned, or almost exactly, not quite her weird vision of me as an electrical engineer and my groom a hydraulic engineer living in a ranch home overlooking the Shasta Dam. Catch-22 is I could never find that joy unless I got far enough away from her that she wouldn't know. Instead, I'm still on the stairs at the window, in the Resistance, tapping my code toward something far under the water.

Snowflakes

There are simpler ways, of course, than convincing the FBI to admit me to the Witness Protection Program, moving to the Aleutian Islands and learning scrimshaw, or killing myself. I could get a new job. At least that would get me away from David and his interminable crosswords. Alice, what's a three-letter word for half a dance? Can, you idiot, *can*. What's a three-letter word for a big heart?

I *aced* the typing test a couple weeks ago when, in fact, I did go for an interview, but other than that, it did not go well. I had to talk to a big-boned redhead who asked me about my education. She said she was impressed by my education, but that seemed to mean that in her experience people who read a lot of fiction will climb out and clean pigeon shit off a window ledge on the 21st floor. They'll walk the boss's Shih Tzu.

When the big-boned redhead asked, as they always do, how I work under pressure, I suspect she wanted to tease out what I'd do if the Shih Tzu peed on the boss's Art Deco rug. I suspect she may have confronted that scenario herself at some point in her career and emerged triumphant, Venus from the sea, a box of cornstarch in her hand.

I wanted to tell her that the best example of my grace under pressure was sitting in this interview without running into the hall screaming, breaking the glass on the fire extinguisher with my bare, small-boned hands, and running back to extinguish her fucking flaming red hair. But you put out a fire from the base, don't you, so before I could subdue the hair shooting from her head like solar flares, I'd have to aim the foam down and drench her French pumps.

I wanted to tell her about the time I'd knocked David off his chair with a toner cartridge and sat at his desk so I could finish a job where he'd fucked up the footnotes. Instead I just smiled and told her that the one thing I liked about my current job was that it was not stressful. I knew I was damning myself but it was worth it to see the look of shock pass over her face like a shooting star—not shock but *envy*—before she stood and extended her big-boned hand to me.

There are circles in hell, and I'd found someone below mine. We both may be dishwater spiraling down a kitchen drain, but I could see a glimmer of greasy light above and she was under me in that curve of cast iron so aptly called the trap. When I got home I wrote a thank-you letter to Ms. Bones that explained everything, though I never sent it.

This morning, Ms. Bones, I managed to put on my skirt without taking the scissors out of my desk and slicing its ruffles into rags—no, into snowflakes, like children make. You remember how magical it is. Simply by folding a piece of paper, you free yourself to cut as messily as you want, and when you unfold the paper, the chaos is symmetrical. The trick is trusting the process. Children who cut tidy, careful lines make boring snowflakes. But that's not quite true. The trick is also knowing how to make the fold, and that's what I've never understood. I just cut. That's how I manage, Ms. Bones, grace under pressure. I just cut.

Jury

Would I be convicted by a jury of my peers? The idea of finding twelve people like me is ridiculous. Where would you look, a limestone cave? I've heard about the primitive men, and women too, who painted bison, reindeer, and even human hands, but I've never heard about anyone who just looked. Find me a Paleolithic woman who went off by herself and looked at the hands painted on a cave wall and wept. She can be on my jury.

Find me the woman who watched a man painting a boar and then reached into the fire, picked up a smoldering hunk of charcoal, walked up to her shadow on the cave wall, and began to paint her own hand. That was a more historic moment than the discovery of fire.

Do they allow convicted felons on juries? I want the Bird Man of Alcatraz, and maybe a shoplifter, a girl who's stolen a silk scarf from Saks and knows beauty isn't a luxury: you've got as much right to it as a hungry man has to steal a can of beans, the good kind baked with molasses. I want everyone: the butcher, the baker, the circuit breaker. The pallbearer, the sun starer, the system error.

I want the girl who sat every Monday afternoon for six years on Mrs. Chen's chenille couch waiting for her piano lesson, listening to Billy Milton finish off Rachmaninov.

I want someone on my jury who had eleven treatments of shock therapy, who had a doctor kick their Coke machine eleven times while they were asleep to see what flavor would explode when they woke and, yes, sometimes it's a good one, sometimes it's a sunset in Maui or getting dressed in the morning without howling. I want more than a Maui sunset. I want a sky. I want a horizon line.

Of My Peers

Juror No. 1: Conceived in a Murphy bed a block from the Boardwalk, the silence in the room covered up by the screams from the Rotor, the simple, elegant ride that went nowhere, an enormous barrel that spun so centrifugal force pinned the riders and they faced one another across an abyss when the floor dropped away.

Juror No. 2: Never traveled outside the continental United States. No, Your Honor, never eaten even one of the seven moles of Oaxaca on the zócalo. Never seen the stick-figure petroglyphs within walking distance of the parking lots on the Kona Coast. Never seen an iguana or an albatross on the Galápagos Islands. Never drunk a Manhattan in a Shanghai speakeasy. I hear they call it a Rio there.

Juror No. 3: Sang alto in the choir of Calvary Episcopal Church: "Now, My Tongue, the Myst'ry Telling." Had to stop after developing vertigo, the interweaving harmonies swaying like an Inca rope bridge over the Urubamba River, the wind playing a terrifying, chromatic accompaniment.

Juror No. 4: Inarticulate as rain falling on benches overrun with morning glory. Makes no distinction between vine and stone, the goldfish and the lily pond, the living and the dead, none of them expressing an opinion either.

Juror No. 5: Confused by sex, its untranslatability. A Romance language speaker who found that everyone else spoke Natchez or Korean or one of those African languages with clicks. Pursued by men clicking in a recess of the mouth she didn't possess, men whose attempts at communication sounded like Tuvan throat singing when they became aroused and expected her to respond in kind.

Juror No. 6: Declared a danger to self and others. Concurred. Extensive voir dire unable to elicit the name of anyone *not* a danger to self and others. Betrayed. A fish that always leapt toward a sun that looked glorious from beneath the surface, an enormous cloud of red krill or bloody chum, then flopped on the deck of a rusted fishing boat, anonymous, gutted, frozen.

Juror No. 7: Cheated on by his wife with their CPA, with the balloon-animal maker at their son's birthday party, the usher at the opera who led them to their seats with his slender flashlight, the Korean grocer who always had the freshest produce (juicy limes, unbelievable plums), the kid who scooped ice cream at Baskin-Robbins (Baskin-Robbins!), the man with a shaven head and a clipboard who rang their doorbell soliciting for Greenpeace, the mayor of Daly City, the Dalai Lama.

Juror No. 8: Had a dozen orgasms in twenty-four hours while studying for her real estate license. It was the taboo, the need to think of nothing but real estate—trying to not think of a pink panther until walls, chairs, everything was pink. The duller the topic, the greater the excitement: adverse possession, eminent domain, yield spread, closing costs. Right of exclusion, right of enjoyment, right of survivorship, right of control.

Juror No. 9: Hospitalized for depression. Hospitalized for psychosis. Don't you dare peel it. Don't you dare sign it. You've written outside the lines. Don't you dare decant the wine. You've spilled it on your white shirt. Don't you dare clean it. Don't you dare take it off. *Take it off.* Don't you dare wear it. *Wear it.*

Juror No. 10: Learned an entire life strategy one morning examining a shell on Morro Bay at low tide: the external deep blue whorls look like the ocean to predators above; the pearly underside looks like the sky to predators below.

Juror No. 11: Alchemist, beekeeper, cutpurse, dog-breaker, eremite, fence, goldbeater, herbalist, interpreter, jack, knacker, lensgrinder, matador, numerologist, orderly, percussionist, quarryman, radiologist, sacristan, time-keeper, underwriter, vintner, wrangler, xenophobe, yeoman, zealot.

Juror No. 12: Autopsy performed by pathologist inconclusive. No residue on hands; no powder. Weighed, measured, photographed from every angle, scanned with ultraviolet light. Birthmark above left scapula. Chest opened from neck to pubis: minimal bleeding. Heart examined in situ: no abnormalities. Brain examined in situ: no signs of violence or any trauma, not a hint, not a hieroglyph.

Alternate No. 1: Experienced joy on several occasions though no record was kept, but why would it. Returned to Seattle one winter on Amtrak, awake all night through the deliriously nameless snow of the Cascades until an apple tree appeared in a field across from the station where the train stopped before dawn.

Alternate No. 2: Burned through ten thousand acres and still not contained. Aided by darkness and wind. Through cedar and pine, ceremony and prayer. Burned through edge, burned through air. Burned through who what when why where. And the seething sea ceaseth and sufficeth us.

II

Shot in the Dark

I promised myself not to exaggerate. I don't want to overreact to what is, after all, a stressful but only rarely catastrophic event in the life of a typical 21st-century employee. It's not as if I have cancer. More like when my doctor told me I have borderline high blood pressure and need to cut back on Chinese food. He didn't know I never eat Chinese food. He was taking a shot in the dark.

When people jump from the Golden Gate, they invariably face the city lights, but what are the statistics when they shoot themselves? What percent do it in the dark? It's not as if you need light to put a muzzle in your maw. How many do it outdoors at night? Near the ocean the sound would be muffled. It would almost be nonviolent. It would be in black-and-white, blood the black ink of calligraphy brushed on the sand, bold strokes forming the Chinese character for home, the ink black except for the red seal the calligrapher signs his name with.

What happened is this: this morning Fran put me on probation. She said there'd been more complaints about my work. About the fact that I wasn't doing it. She asked if I had anything to say. I did not. Call me Jesus. Actually Jesus had a lot to say. Call me the Holy Ghost. Tongues of flame. I would have spoken in tongues if I'd dared. Fran wouldn't have known what hit her. *Talitha koum.* Little girl, arise.

Nothing is as beautiful as fire. Because it contains all colors. Because it dances with seven veils. Because it crosses the seven gates to the underworld. Because it drops a veil at each gate. Because it is the way and the truth. Period. Because it asked for the head of the Baptist. Because its secret name is Isis and it danced at the crucifixion.

I sat in Fran's office counting the items of clothing I wore. Seven. Perfect. Enough to pay my way to the underworld. In college a girl took off her clothes under the quince tree in the quad and walked to class. Everyone figured she was crazy. A campus cop led her away and came back later and folded her clothes.

Fran gave me three months to "change course," as if I were an oil tanker or the *QE2.* She assured me this would be kept between the two of us. She knew I'd hate that more than any discipline she could think up with her clever brain. And I knew she must have "consulted" with David about me. Somehow, when I wasn't paying attention, they'd become friends. Now I recalled them talking in the hall about their favorite dishes. That's what did it. My God, walnut pesto.

Nevertheless, I did not slip off my blue shoes and point them at Fran's heart. I did not unbuckle my matching blue belt and hang it on the ficus in the hall. And I would wait until I got home to take off my blouse and skirt and burn them in the bear-claw bathtub like an offering to Isis, fire to fire. I know that sounds crazy, but it would do no one any harm, would it? And there are very few options I have left that would do no one any harm.

Capital Punishment

Does it deter *anyone*? Of course for some it would be a reward, but I'm talking about the process. To be, for years, a cause célèbre, journalists like Truman Capote wanting to investigate how your mind works as if your head were a cuckoo clock but made in the U.S.A., its lack of Swiss precision made up for by its Rube Goldberg weirdness.

And the *worst*-case scenario—what happens if you exhaust all your appeals—is a candlelight vigil by hundreds of strangers outside San Quentin. It's a lot more than show up when Joan Q. Citizen gets the flu and croaks at home.

More than showed up ten years ago when I cut myself for the first time: there was no vigil then. But the truth is: it felt good, and half the thrill was that *someone would clean up after me*. From the time you're three you expend Herculean amounts of energy cleaning up after yourself in every sense: physical, emotional, and spiritual. I knew my mother wouldn't let me go home from the hospital with bloodstains still on my white, hexagonal bathroom tile.

I couldn't tell an artery from a vein if, well, my life depended on it, but I know the blood from a vein is dark scarlet as it flows into the heart. Blood from an artery is bright crimson as it bursts out, and crimson is what first responders dread. I was scarlet: I'd be okay.

The other half of the thrill was how easy it was. Itzhak Perlman practiced four hours a day for ten years, with *polio*, before he debuted at Carnegie Hall. Margot Fonteyn practiced for decades before she danced *Giselle* with Nureyev and almost danced him to death. I made the same point in twenty minutes when I was twenty-four, in a studio apartment, with no practice at all.

What does it mean to *mean* something? Did Picasso *mean* it? All those flesh tones and sharp angles. Did Mozart mean *The Marriage of Figaro*? Isn't man the only animal who does *not* always mean it? Did Mom and Dad mean it when they said they loved me? Did they mean it when they said they loved each other?

Sometimes suicide is nothing more than a way of saying "No, actually I was not being ironic. I meant it." Even then people think you're being operatic. Of course you are. You have to get the audience's attention, so busy in the upper balcony unwrapping their lemon drops. Sometimes you have to raise your eyebrows to a theatrical height and wear lilac eye shadow with black mascara, gold glitter on red gloss, just to get someone to listen.

The Carrier

No one knows, but I've been carrying. Yes, like a virus, or an unborn child. I put it in my purse a month ago and haven't touched it since. Well, I've *touched* it, to make sure it's there. It's wrapped in a red scarf, buried under the Kleenex and lipstick and other crap on the one-in-a-million chance Fran opens my purse to look for a tampon or a bobby pin. Buried under a map of the Paris Metro and Père Lachaise where I marked the niche with Isadora Duncan's ashes.

I like to carry a lot of maps. This morning I added the Vatican, not the tourist highway to the Sistine Chapel, but the forgotten paths to Isis and Osiris. Cleopatra's bust in the Vatican basement is exactly as explosive as the double-action matte-silver revolver in my purse as I ride home on the 19 Polk bus.

Carrying a concealed weapon (without the permit they'd never grant me, of course) is the opposite of being naked. As God transmutes Himself into a crust of bread—as the genie *longs* to be stoppered in an aromatic oil lamp—I pour my soul into a smooth-handled .38.

Flesh is vulnerable. That's the meaning of a gun: not the protection it offers your flesh directly, but the security it gives you of a place to store your soul in a steel case separate from your body. It's not sexual, but it has a similar intensity. Sometimes the whole universe disappears except for your body or someone else's body or one part of your body. As the saying goes, *it all comes down to this.* It all comes down to a bridge over a pond or perhaps a farmhouse window glimpsed through wisteria. It all comes down to whether the one person you love among all the judges and junk bond dealers in the world is fucking someone else. It all comes down to a gun in your hand.

Knowing matters: knowing that when the frizzy-haired man with the briefcase sits next to you on the bus when there are empty rows, you could end his life. Knowing that when the hostess at Pierre's Bistro seats you next to the condiment station, you could end her life.

It matters, but sometimes that's not enough. It's good to know you've invested your savings wisely, but sometimes you have to liquidate. Sometimes you have to cash out.

The Abyssal Plain of the Sea

Everything was fine between David and me until Fran interfered. It sounds crazy but it's true. Our problems didn't have anything to do with David's amicable wife or his anorexic divorce or his pet Abyssinian named after that movie star, not Meryl but . . . Streep. He'd call her from his porch at night: *Streep!*

David and I would have worked it out. But Fran got jealous that every month or two David and I would share a scoop of blueberry yogurt at our desks and talk about public television. She set out to destroy that and she did. Burned the ships and razed the city and buried it in salt like Rome did to Carthage in the Punic Wars.

Fran is smart. She has the sort of intelligence that stupid people excel at. She knows how to find someone's weak spot and apply pressure. As they tell you in first aid, in case of bleeding, apply pressure. She hints that she knows your secrets without telling you which, so you tell her your mother's maiden name, Fleming, and then the name of your first pet, your German Shepherd, Buff, and finally you tell her about meeting David on the weekend for waffles and fig jam.

The ending of *Titanic*: the old woman drops her blue diamond into the ocean. The worst ending ever. Why would she do that? To show that she didn't need *things* anymore? But people need things. Secret things. That's why we evolved with our hearts inside our bodies, not dangling like dicks. The way they hang like exposed wires or clock pendulums explains a lot about men. Maybe everything. How they act as if they're the victim while they bury you in salt.

How is it, then, that the world still seems beautiful? Even to me. And there's no cynicism in that *seems*. It's not because God made the world beautiful. It's because of all the coal-black secrets people have taken to their graves and that have hardened into diamond underground.

There's a story in my family that my grandmother and her brother-in-law were in love, and my mother was the daughter of her uncle. When I was a girl the four of them played bridge after the supper of short ribs and egg noodles my mother cooked for them. When my grandmother was dying, my mother begged her for the truth, but Grandma lay in her bed and gritted her teeth.

Grandma meant there are limits to what a child can ask of its mother, just as there are to what a mother can ask of her child. A mother can't ask her child not to cancel her vote, for example, by casting her ballot for the other party even if that party is opposed to every value the mother cherishes, not even if the child is casting her *life* for the other party. As I did.

The earth glows with an underground autumn of golds, copper and bronze from all the mysteries people have borne with them into its crust. The ocean would be a paler, more watery hue, not its deep cobalt blue, if not for all the dreams hidden in the mollusks and red corals on what biologists aptly call the abyssal plain of the sea.

White Noise

It seems years since I got David's Christmas card with the Chinese landscape, but it was four months ago. By then we weren't speaking. I've kept it propped against the toaster on my kitchen table. A fire hazard, I know. The "snow" is gold leaf, and I've studied it but can't figure out how the artist lets you know that the gold is snow. The tigers are partially "submerged" in the gold, so you know it's not a gold-paved courtyard in the emperor's palace, and the tigers don't seem to be swimming: they don't have that earnest look. They look at ease, the way you would if your home were a mountain of gold snow and you wore a gold coat and you had never seen a human being.

I like having the card on the table next to the cutting board, where I've never sliced so much as a tomato, when I eat my chili or ginger noodles. I hardly ever look at it. I just like its white noise. I've always thought that if I decide to do *it*, one of my last acts would be to burn the card, but that seems melodramatic, although the gold snow in flames would be beautiful. I'll probably just toss it. I like the idea of it buried in a landfill next to the disposable pink razor I shave my legs with on the last day of my life.

I'd say it was a love letter, or a reasonable facsimile. At least David seemed to mean what he said, and meaning what you say to someone is, I think, pretty much what it means to love someone.

December 14, 2007

Dear Alice,

I hope you won't mind my writing. I'm not sure why you don't want to talk to me anymore. If I've done anything to hurt you, I'm sorry. Getting to know you has meant a lot to me and I hope we can be friends again, but it's all right if you don't want to. I don't want you to feel uncomfortable around me. I care about you. I hope you have a good Christmas.

David

P.S. Let me try again. Alice, I'm sorry. I love you and I'm sorry I haven't covered the stairs leading up to your apartment with flowers, all the state flowers that are illegal to pick, from Arkansas apple blossoms to Wisconsin violets, and wine barrels full of the California poppies that flood the deserts from the Mojave to the Anza-Borrego. I'm sorry I didn't build an ice sculpture of the Taj Mahal in your parking lot on a hot summer day so you could walk beneath its dome and feel the rain as it almost evaporated before it touched your skin. I'm sorry I didn't rewrite the lyrics of "Maria" for "Alice" and hire a trio of Plácido Domingo, Lou Reed, and Howlin' Wolf to serenade you. I'm sorry I didn't tell you I loved you the way ribs love vinegar and smoke, the way a match loves dark rum on peaches, the way monsoons love the South China Sea, tornadoes love Oklahoma, and earthquakes love the Rim of Fire.

I'm sorry I didn't tell you sooner that I love you.

David

Nothing at all mystical has ever happened to me: no rose lights gleaming in a corner of my bedroom above the oak desk, no visions of the sky suddenly opening like an orchid, no Jesus walking on Monterey Bay at dusk, walking out of the water onto the sand, disappearing into an alley off Figueroa strewn with broken glass and bougainvillea, although there was a time I prayed for a sign like that. I prayed for more than a sign: I prayed for a mark, for a bruise.

It's strange, considering all the voices I've heard: I've never heard God's. It's always the PG&E man, or my kindergarten teacher, Miss Bliss, or Mom telling me I'm dressed all wrong for my debut. Still, I believe other people have seen the rose lights they claim to have seen. Why not? I believe Mr. Warnick when he says the mangoes are ripe at Wen Ho's. Is that any different?

I believe more people have seen Jesus on Figueroa Street than have had someone say something to them and mean it. I did not see *The Light* when I read David's letter, but it would be fair to say I saw the light. It was shining weakly on the kitchen table when I read the mail on a late Saturday afternoon, and the weakness allowed me to see the other colors shot through it, burgundies and ochres and blues. It was shining on the toaster and the cutting board, and on the half slice of bread I'd left on the counter that morning, and on the wood floor and its water stains by the window where the rains had come in for a hundred years, and on a corner of the blue jute rug I got at Cost Plus, the sharp edge between light and shadow becoming more and more smudged as the sun went down.

By the time the sun *had* gone down, I knew two things: I knew that something had changed forever, and I knew that David and I would still not speak on Monday morning, except for the curt good mornings that had become our routine and in fact have remained our routine. How could it have gone on so long? It's Easter week now. But how could it end? The paradox is absolute. David knows me deeply and doesn't know me at all. Even God had to submit to that paradox and split Himself into Father and Son, the Unknown and the Known. One can't exist without the other. I think I would explode . . . no, I think I would turn into snow, snow so light it would disintegrate before it ever touched the earth, if I revealed any more of myself to David. I would only be revealing the parts of myself that are *not me*. That seems to be what the world calls honesty.

I don't trust God anymore. If I know anything, if there's one lesson every moment of my life has conspired to teach me, it's that power and love are incompatible. Why would anyone think God is the one exception to that rule?

Shadow Play

It's Easter Sunday night and I haven't slept since Thursday unless I've been walking in my sleep, which is possible. I walked the two miles to work on Friday because I didn't expect to come home and I wanted to see everything. The rain gutters, the maze of wires electrifying the trolleys, the mulberry trees lining the sidewalk. See them for the first time. It felt as if people were seeing *me* for the first time. I felt like the *Taxi Driver* guy. You lookin' at me? Or more as if I was wearing Jodie Foster's white hat and Robert De Niro was looking at *me*.

I should have felt wracked under the circumstances, but at the stop where I'd caught the bus for eight years all I saw was Red Rock Realty painted in black on the bench. It was earlier than usual so I didn't recognize anyone. A thin, thin-lipped man who looked like the old guy in *A Hard Day's Night* had taken the place of the curly-haired woman I'd thought was a florist because she always looked in bloom. A girl toting a backpack covered with travel stickers to places she probably wanted to see—Nepal, Budapest, Fiji—had taken the place of the teenage boy none of us dared ask to turn his music down. They did seem to have taken the places of the regulars, but only because they were at the stop earlier.

I saw things I'd never noticed from the bus. A brass plaque on Russian Hill in memory of Russian sailors. I'd never known the hill was named for a cemetery that no longer exists but was once at the summit, where penthouses now float with panoramic views. Someone must be buried under every square foot of the city, but the land is so valuable now that one brass plaque must do for a hundred sailors.

San Francisco is unique, but it's also like every other town, and I'd never seen that before so clearly. It's home to nail salons and coffee shops, though in Dubuque you might be less likely to find the Thai woman who opens the blinds to the nail salon as she flicks her cigarette to the sidewalk, or the coffeehouse owner who brings out from behind the counter for his oldest friends the grimy bottle of grappa that isn't on the menu, or the brisk walk of the man in the gray suit who crosses the street and goes into the Indonesian consulate half-hidden by a stand of poplars.

I imagined an inner conference room in the consulate where shadow puppets performed by the light of an oil lamp. The audience had sat on the floor all night—nine hours!—watching, listening to gamelan music. That is a commitment that families watching *Cats* at the Curran can't even imagine. But I'm imagining what went on in a building behind poplars. More likely the consulate clerks were doing what I do at my job: figuring out whether to feed a letter face up or face down into the fax machine.

But I do imagine . . . I want someone to sit in an inner room at three in the morning watching a shadow play of a green-eyed girl abducted in the woods by an old king. He holds her prisoner until she forgets it's a prison and forgets her brown-eyed lover (all this done with shadows), until one day her lover goes hunting. The audience waits to see if the two will recognize each other, even though they know—they've heard the story a thousand times—when she pours the mint tea he'll see the scar on her wrist from when the king's guard seized her years before. They want to hear it again and again: it was her scar that saved her.

Collateral Damage

I didn't realize it was *Good* Friday until I passed the church in Washington Square and saw an altar boy carrying boxes of lilies into the basement. I guess the church has to keep flowers hidden until Easter. At least they don't pluck out the pistils and stamens like the Victorians did. They want the lilies to erupt from the altar on Easter Sunday like Dolly Parton from a birthday cake, strumming her guitar, singing "Jolene."

All it meant to me was that my elaborate planning had been in vain: the office would close early. Fran had timed it so the end of my probation would coincide with the Resurrection. She had no ambivalence about power. I realized it had been her all along—her and the other Frans of the world—who had come and were coming and would always come between the Davids and me.

I'd planned to wait until everyone had left—everyone but her: she always worked late. It wouldn't be easy but I'd rehearsed. I'd practiced taking the gun from my purse in the elevator of my apartment building in the time it took to rise to the third floor. The elevator walls are mirrors, and trust me, I did not look like Robert De Niro. I looked ridiculous.

Sometimes the simplest mechanics of everyday life overwhelm me. I shrug to adjust my shoulder strap so I can unclasp my purse and find the keys to unlock my door with the hand that's holding my mail while my other arm holds a bag of groceries. Now: which hand turns on the light? It's no surprise that it complicates matters to add a gun to the mix. I'd have to improvise, and that's not my forte.

What always happens in the movies—whether it's *Bonnie and Clyde* or *Crime and Punishment*—is that the wrong characters get killed. Lizaveta of the soulful eyes and Russian crucifix, tall as a basketball center, gets killed. The inevitability of collateral damage. For a thousand years it was the sign that an act was evil. The *mark*.

The acceptance of collateral damage is the hallmark of our time, as omnipresent as Diet Coke. The doves protest it in Afghanistan—*because they don't care* if portraits of Osama bin Laden are hung on the walls of Kabul—but they accept it like everyone else when something they care about is at stake.

I have a zero-tolerance policy toward collateral damage. I've *been* collateral damage. I've been the dove. On my walk to the office I saw a Ho Chi Minh lookalike enter the library with a newspaper under his arm, I saw a stockbroker gulp a cappuccino on his way downtown, I saw a nun in a school playground get her flash cards ready for class. I wouldn't hurt them, even though they took for granted an almost animal joy I'll never know. The cat leaps and falls back to the sun-warmed earth with a mouthful of blue feathers. Joy is distributed as unequally in this world as love or money.

I was recalibrating my plan of action to ensure there would be no collateral damage, just two neat bullets in Fran's chest and one in mine. I would walk into her office and shut the door as if I wanted to have a "heart to heart," which in a way I did, and she would be smug with pride that she had shepherded me into a state where I was ready to confess.

Bless me, Fran, for I have sinned. Yea, I hath taken long lunch hours. I hath procrastinated in the production of documents. I hath sabotaged the laser printer. I hath been sarcastic in my communion with my coworkers. And yea, I hath brought a lethal weapon into the workplace with intent to inflict bodily and spiritual harm on persons who toil with me in the vineyard—on you, Fran.

I wouldn't give her the satisfaction. She would ask, *What is truth, Alice?* as if she were Pontius Pilate or Professor Pompous in Philosophy 101, and I would shoot her in the heart or as close to it as I could get with my presumably moist, trembling hands. It would be close enough, and if not, it would certainly surprise her enough to allow me to get off a second, final shot. Next to final.

History was on my side. I knew I'd be ham-handed, but no more so than the millions of soldiers who'd managed despite their bungling to kill one another at Borodino, Gettysburg, Fallujah. They did it the same way I would, the old-fashioned way, one by one.

Songbird

I know about the plans of men, but the beauty of *my* plan was that *whether or not* it went awry, the next step was the same: to turn the gun on myself. The hours I spent deciding where to point it! I was afraid I'd miss my heart, or that my heart would survive like a hunk of uranium ore with a half-life of 700,000,000 years.

I could aim at my temple, but I wanted to hold the revolver with both hands. Besides, it's always the "commander of the regiment" in old movies who withdraws into his study with its globe and leather-bound books and a decanter of sherry to shoot himself in the temple. It looks as if he's saluting.

I thought of aiming between my eyes. This sounds strange, but I love myself too much. I love myself. You can't shoot someone you love in the face. I also happen to believe, and for similar reasons, you can't cremate someone you love, and I knew that's what Mom and Dad would do with me as soon as they heard. We'd like the check *now*, please, waiter. We have tickets for the theater: *Jersey Boys*.

Yes, vanity is a factor, but is it wrong that it crossed my mind David might be a witness? There would be confusion, people rushing to the windows to see if shots had been fired in the street below or a truck had backfired. David would be the one to notice that Fran was missing and her door was shut, and with one of his infuriating intuitions he'd open the door.

He'd have no perspective at first: the black plastic nameplate on Fran's desk and the red spiral vase on her desk with the single sunflower would seem, for a moment, of equal significance to the body slumped on her desk, and the other body on the floor by the yellow umbrella she kept for emergencies.

I settled on a shot into the mouth as the best option, aimed at my brain *stem*. You win the giant panda if you hit the medulla oblongata. The idea is to sever the *link* between the brain and the heart, which seems to be the source of my problems anyway.

I couldn't predict how I would fall, but I imagined something like fainting, Fay Wray in *King Kong*. Unrealistic, but I wanted to be beautiful for David. No, not *for* him. I wanted my beauty to stun him—to give him a seizure so he'd choke on his tongue when he saw me.

It was unlikely, I knew, that I'd fall in perfect Anna Pavlova form as a dying swan, my blood a dark fall of hair on my shoulders, but that was my hope, that or flat on my back with a thin line of blood trailing from the corner of my mouth as if I'd swallowed one of those rare French songbirds, ortolans, that gourmets trap in the vineyards of Bordeaux, dredge in brandy, and eat whole with one swift crunch, while they drape linen napkins over their heads to trap the aroma—and to hide their ecstasy from God.

I'm Not There

Needless to say, that's not how it worked out. When I got to work on Friday, I finished my coffee in the token park some corporation had been forced to install in return for a permit to construct thirty stories of HVAC and concrete. Well, it's not as if I could have survived in any other "environment." I wouldn't last a week as a waitress, let alone a park ranger or a marine biologist.

I sat under a redwood and looked up through the branches at my office windows on the 21st floor and felt vertigo, as if my body didn't fit, as if it were off-kilter, a pair of itchy pantyhose twisted around my soul.

My plan was to work the morning as if everything was normal until the office thinned out at noon when people left for Good Friday services. We had more than our share of Catholics. On Ash Wednesday half the office wore those smudges on their foreheads that are meant to be a cross but are like one of those dots Indian women wear that look more like curry powder. You'd think priests would apply the ash with care, but it must be an assembly line to them. Once I saw Good Friday services at Carmel Mission, and at one point the choir sang memorably, *Someday you'll find that I'm not there*, as if God were Hank Williams.

The morning at work was *not* memorable, but David acted strange, as if he suspected. I heard Fran and her doe-eyed henchgirl Dee laughing, and if it wasn't at me, that was only by chance. David was like a bad extra in a movie trying to look as if he's just hanging his trench coat on a hook when you know he's aware of the camera. Did he notice me carry my purse everywhere? Usually I sling it under my desk as if I could care less if the FedEx man takes it.

Funny: I remember seeing a FedEx *girl* do the pickup that day. Maybe our regular guy is Catholic. The stack of boxes on her cart was taller than she was, but she was not the type to let anything slow her down. She was like Sherman on the march to Savannah. As was I.

Rainforest

All things considered, I was calm. At ten I took my break and read the newspaper at my desk. I honestly felt as if I didn't have a care in the world. By eleven the adrenalin had kicked in as if I'd gone to drink at a river and seen the reflection of a sabertooth next to me: green eyes shimmering in green water.

Sabertooth tigers once were *all over* California. The throat of a white-tailed deer was slit by a crescent moon. I was at its mercy. But what was *it*? Whatever it was, I sat at my desk as long as I could bear it, afraid of disturbing it, but as Cro-Magnon man had to back away quietly from the water, I had to go for a walk.

It was unprecedented for me to be gone from my desk at eleven o'clock. I walked the Financial District, under the trusses of the Transamerica Pyramid, and felt as if I were—not in a jungle—a rainforest. My concentration for that half hour was as sharply focused as it's ever been. I walked as if I might step on a venomous ribbon vanishing in liana vines, or fall into a trap dug for feral pigs, or simply *lose my way.*

The flashes of beauty that flit through my peripheral vision and hearing and smell were all the more intense because I couldn't stop. A semi screeched as it parked to deliver furniture on Icehouse Alley: a cockatoo cried, flashing its red coverts from a treetop in the canopy. The scent of stir-fried garlic overflowed from a Chinese restaurant preparing for the lunch rush: ylang-ylang flowers flung their intoxicating aroma, strewn to prepare a bed for newlyweds. Two women in black and yellow coats strolled into a bakery: a tiger stole into the forest with too much dignity to look back for predators, and I followed his path.

As the saying goes, the die was cast. Didn't Caesar say that when he led his army across the river? We forget that he wasn't heading into the unknown. He said it when he began the march *back* toward Rome. I always thought it meant playing dice, trusting to a game of chance, but now I wondered if it meant die *casting*, pouring molten lead into molds of letters to print Shakespeare or the Bible. "Tomorrow and tomorrow and tomorrow." "Tomorrow will I bring the locusts into thy coast." *Into thy coast*. That always scared the shit out of me.

In other words, as I crossed the border of Chinatown into Jackson Square, I realized it meant the opposite of what I thought. Casting the die is precisely *not* trusting chance. The shift in my understanding of that phrase captures perfectly the shift in my understanding of everything. I turned and walked back toward the office. The letterpress. Hot metal. Movable type. Offset. The die was cast.

The Wooden Horse

It's a curious fact of modern urban life that the social encounter one is most likely to have on the street is with the homeless. Who else will talk to you? Maybe if you get an apple fritter every morning for a year at Didi's Donuts, Didi will nod, almost imperceptibly, if you run into her on the sidewalk. Probably not.

In any case no one spoke to me on Friday morning. Years ago a man on the corner offered to sing "Moon River" to me for twenty dollars and I fell for it, and we both kept up our ends of the deal, which is more than you can say for most interactions. He had a good voice.

I'm just saying sometimes I wish an ordinary Joe or Joan would ask me for directions to the Ferry Building, or tell me my boots are hot (which they are), or point out Venus in the morning sky and tell me how Lincoln's inauguration came to a halt as the crowd paused to marvel at Venus, not knowing what it was, and then my Joe would look at me as if to say he'd known I was the kind of person who'd appreciate that story and he'd just wanted to confirm his intuition. It might have made a difference if anyone had said, just once, something like that to me. David came the closest. It wasn't love at first or five hundredth sight, but when I met him, I saw his wound right away, maybe larger than mine. Not the sort of wound you get when someone has hurt you. The sort you get when no one has loved you enough to hurt you.

I met David's parents once. Well, I saw them once when they were waiting in the lobby to take him out for lunch. It was right after he and Janette had separated, and they were worried about him. They hadn't warned him they were coming because his mother thought (accurately) he might have made up an excuse to avoid them. All in all, she seemed to be a very accurate woman. I followed him out to the lobby so I could see them, and he shook his father's hand and then shook his mother's hand and they went out for sushi.

That's the sort of wound I mean. Not really a wound. Something like the paleness of your skin if you've been locked in a dark room all your life, like Kaspar Hauser, with nothing but a wooden horse. Sunlight—the thing you want most—will sear your flesh if you encounter it. The horse was bare wood, but if it had been gold with a crimson mane, Kaspar Hauser would never have known. The mild sunlight everyone takes for granted—the girl scraping out a sandcastle's moat, the old man in the park sleeping as the sun rockabyes him—would incinerate you. To have been not-loved with such consistency, such dogged *faithfulness*, that now any love at all is unbearable.

The Light of Reason

When I got back from my "breather," David was gone, another twist to disrupt my plans. He never took an early lunch or left early on Fridays. His absence actually could have made things easier, if only I'd known whether he was coming back. And then Fred came in—one of the lawyers I hardly ever see—and he seemed to think it was the perfect time to chat about my Easter plans.

Even in my distracted state, especially in my distracted state, I appreciated his gesture. It was as if he were throwing a life preserver to a chambermaid entombed for a hundred years in an oak-paneled stateroom on the *Titanic*. But that was Fred. Fred is one of those people who genuinely live by the light of reason. Human nature is such a puzzle to him he doesn't judge you if you act strange, because anything anyone does seems strange to him. He actually asked me once if I understood why what's-her-name in *Flashdance* would want to go to dance school when she had a good-paying job as a welder. Fred didn't even understand why E.T. wanted to go home. His exact words to me on the subject were, "Why not just love the one you're with?" And it was an honest question.

Even if I had to wonder if he made his wife nervous, flirting was the last thing on Fred's mind. He may be the only man I'd be comfortable with no matter what. If we were working late and he took me for oysters and champagne at Chez Robert, it would mean he felt like a bite to eat.

Not like David. Nothing like David. David can't give me one of the extra ketchup packets from his snack to-go without acting as if both of us should make the sign of the cross and genuflect at the consecration: *This is my blood.* I don't mind that David is too romantic to see the light of reason, but he's proud of it, like a blind man proud of his hearing. I sat next to a blind man once at the symphony, and he groused all through the second movement. Don't talk to me about the superior hearing of the blind. I know better.

Vessels

Why does a vessel like a vase hold water, but a vessel like a ship is held *by* water? In that case water *is* a vessel. And: blood vessels. And: I am a vessel. A goblet. I could watch someone pouring water from a pitcher all day. The clay pitcher on the sill of my kitchen window. The pattern. The blue glaze. Baked in a kiln, itself a vessel of fire.

What made me think of that? Of course: the ketchup, the consecration, the blood, the chalice. Sometimes I feel as if I'm evaporating, and then David walks into the room and I can feel myself pour back into myself, filling every crevice. And then the glass stopper is put back in as if I were wine or perfume. . . . No, I'm a decanter, not a stopped bottle. That's the beauty of a vessel: it separates *in* from *out* but with an opening.

Once I was walking home at night and glanced into someone's house at the precise moment when I could look through their kitchen, the breadbox shining on the counter, down a pale green hallway dimly lit by a bronze wall sconce, into a bedroom at the end of the hall, and see a woman, laughing or weeping, sitting on the edge of the bed in a blue robe.

Some people are like that house. I wouldn't call David an *open* person. But sometimes the tumblers of the locks click into place and the steel door opens, and I see something in his eyes as if I'm looking back into the cave where the first human being lived a million years ago. Think how he would know *nothing*, not what he looked like or what he *was*. He could be a fish. He could be a river. He wouldn't know if the stars were one thing or separate. That's what it is about David: when the sun goes behind a cloud he looks surprised for a moment as if it's the first time he's seen anything like it.

David has cut me as deeply as it is possible for one person to cut another without killing them. Yet there were moments when I bared my throat to him and his only response was to kiss the pulse under my skin. Metaphorically, maybe, but does that matter? *I love you* is a metaphor.

What I'm trying to say is there were a couple moments with David: awful ones like the afternoon we shared apricot ice cream as we stood at the end of the pier and watched a container ship depart through the Golden Gate bound for Hong Kong, and we were empty and we were *brimming*, but for some ridiculous reason like there were no apricot trees nearby to *resonate*, we didn't do anything. I just gave him my best *We don't need trees* look. *We have wind and water.* And we didn't. And we had.

Apocalypse

There was nothing to do but wait for noon and screw up my courage. How many psychos does it take to screw up their courage? Five: me and the four horsemen of the Apocalypse telling me how. I just had to wait until the launch codes were locked in and I'd be unable to turn back.

Instead, David walked into the room precisely at noon and handed me a squid with writhing red tentacles, and I heard him say, *Happy Easter.* I realized it was a bouquet of tulips, but that was almost more disturbing. It may be hard to believe, but no one had ever given me flowers, and I wonder now if my father had ever given them to my mother. I can't remember fresh flowers in our house. I'd never realized what an effective gesture it is. Catherine of Aragon would have forgiven Henry VIII for Anne Boleyn if he'd given her Spanish roses.

Flowers are, after all, so unlikely. That out of dirt and root and stem is expelled this alien *thing* that could not be further from its origin in texture, color, and form. Nevertheless, did David honestly think I'd forgive him for his months of silence (nothing on this earth matters less than that I started it) if he simply gave me these vortices of flame, whirling with such fury they seemed to be still?

My first impulse was to back away as if they *were* reptilian or even cephalopodan. I looked at the florist's card, three words in David's small, neat handwriting: *O soave fanciulla.* I didn't know whether to lay the card on my tongue like a communion wafer or feed it into the shredder for confidential documents. In the end I simply turned away, and David didn't exactly look hurt when I said *No, thank you*, the first real words I'd said to him in a long time. He looked lost, like someone who just missed the last train out of Bakersfield, the last train *ever* out of Bakersfield.

I confess I tasted a pinch not of satisfaction but relief when I said no to him. It works, I've learned: hurting people. It works, in fact, extraordinarily, exponentially well. You may have been abused your entire life, but if you key an anonymous car (it doesn't have to be a silver BMW; an underpaid overworked kindergarten teacher's old Datsun will do), it will relieve the pain—maybe just for a moment, but sometimes a moment is all you need.

So I said to him a terrible thing, as if I were in a Henry James novel: *People who don't care about each other shouldn't give each other gifts*, and he said, as if he were not in a Henry James novel, *But I do care about you*. It was the way he said it, matter-of-factly, as if he'd said, *But it* is *Tuesday*, or *Quito* is *the capital of Ecuador*, or *I* do *love you*. As if I'd misunderstood the most obvious thing in the world, which I guess I had, and as if it could be corrected with a simple clarification, which it could not.

And that thing that everyone knows in principle but does not know in practice, does not in fact know at all, I suddenly knew. First I knew that it was true of David, and then I knew that it was true of me: that someone who has lied, manipulated, betrayed, and *enjoyed* hurting someone else may at the same time love them with a passion as pure and fierce as the wind that blows in the Kali Gorge at Annapurna.

Kali

Goddess of death, blue-black monsoon, hear my prayer. Not a prayer but a contract, not a contract but an equation. The speed of light squared equals a bullet train to a black hole. It takes one to know one. Kali, call *me*, this time. Your scarab doesn't scare. Your devil's dildo rides thin air. I eat your pale fire. I face off your eclipse. Possess me if you will. Only you know the way in, the password I keep changing. One day through a nick in my eye. The next down my throat like rice wine. Thread me like a wick through a candle. Burn, turn black, if you will. You will only melt my white wax crystal clear.

III

Joe Blow From Kokomo

One prisoner on Alcatraz was in solitary so long he didn't remember his own name and was known as Joe Blow from Kokomo. Joe had a window in his cell no larger than the deck of cards he'd been allowed to play with for seventeen years, the cards' faces rubbed so smooth he could only tell one from another by marks he'd made, biting a notch from one corner of the Jack of Clubs. As he'd aged he'd lost his hearing until he couldn't overhear the guards' gossip any longer or even the other prisoners banging tin cups on the bars.

Years ago, when my plan was to jump from the Bridge, I imagined that I'd face Joe's window and he'd see me fall—what a cacophony of emotions he'd feel. What a riot. The prison was long shut by the time I'd reached that point, and Joseph X. Murphy (someone should remember his name) was long dead, so in fact it would have been an anonymous caretaker, sweating to keep the heavy honeysuckle and sweet pea vines in check on the island, who saw me.

I've been in solitary so long myself, behind so many locks—combination and deadbolt, padlock and latch—that a whole flood of flowers couldn't reach me. David had no way of knowing how much I wanted to be the person who could take them home and bathe with red and gold petals gliding over my skin.

Sometimes I think the universe is evolving toward unutterable grief. No, rather: *utterable* grief. Exactly that.

The grief that I am not that person. Does the hound pause to admire the pheasant's blue plumage before he shuts his jaws on the feathered bones? Human beings invent cosmologies with a complexity to shame an internal combustion engine, all so they can continue their conversation with the dead. I know why that geologist took a rock pick and smashed the *Pietà*.

It's a gift when someone makes you rethink everything: why you don't pray, why you put on shoes in the morning and fasten their small black buckles, why you carry a gun along with your minty gum. Most people on the street go through their lives without questioning their breakfast cereal or vacation spot, let alone their sexual practices or political convictions. Maybe they questioned them when they were eighteen. Then they were done.

David did me a favor. My spree could wait for a day or two while I rethought. When I changed my major from Marine Biology to Comp Lit, I kept rereading the textbook to assure myself I wasn't making a mistake, as if I were visiting an old boyfriend to make sure there was *nothing* I missed, not the ridge on his nose or his vampire jokes. When I read passages like "Dead zones are often caused by the decay of algae during algal blooms," I remembered the part of marine biology I loved, not to mention the possibility it held out of a middle-class income that would allow my children to have the dance lessons I never had.

Dance is different from music. In fact if there's one thing I've learned—and it wasn't an easy lesson. Think of the sixty instruments in Beethoven's Ninth Symphony (that's not even counting the chorus) or the torrents of a Chopin nocturne. Now think of trying to express all that with your feet. With blisters. And if you can't express it with your body, it doesn't mean much, does it?

That's what this is all about, isn't it? This *thing*: this *offing* yourself, polishing yourself off, icing yourself, fragging yourself, blowing yourself away, taking yourself out for a ride, hitting the road with no brakes and no bearings. This pointed question, sharp as a scalpel. To answer it with your body. To express love or hate or *anything* with even the most graceful body is to steer a wheelbarrow full of stones down a rutted mud path after a hurricane.

It felt as if David had ripped out those tulips by their roots. I could almost see the scraggly bulbs still pumping with the force that had given as much as the blooms could absorb and wanted to return to the earth. I couldn't look at David anymore without seeing the seething entrails of his marriage dragging behind him, trailing its fibrous, mucky rootlets. I knew that in some demented way he'd left Janette for me, and that was the one gift, red and wet and raw as a squalling newborn, I could never accept.

Exhibits

If only he would have said my name. But I do care about you, *Alice*. My name melting like snow on his tongue until he breathed it out in a white cloud and I saw it whole. I left him holding the stalks and took the elevator down twenty-one floors and did not look back until I got home and shut the door of my apartment. I had to wait for the bus and it was a long five minutes. As it arrived, David ran up the sidewalk to catch me before I climbed on—but of course it wasn't him. It was a red-faced attorney carrying a briefcase who looked nothing like David and I wanted to take my gorgeous gun out of my purse and shoot him for being David and then shoot him for not being David.

It probably didn't even occur to him that he didn't have to stand in the hall like a coat rack holding a bouquet until some paralegal walked by and he could explain, I got these for Alice and *the crazy bitch wouldn't take them*. I'm sure he said I got these for Alice *for Easter*, as if getting one's coworker flowers for Easter was the conventional, *normal* thing to do, as if it wasn't anything personal.

Heroes always say anyone would have done the same thing. The desire to be normal is that strong. The gas meter reader who went into a burning building and saved a woman's life never says he was taking his time reading her meter hoping to catch a glimpse of her legs through the curtains as she put on her baby-blue underwear the way he'd seen her once before—putting it on quickly, recklessly, as if she was late for work, the little hop to keep her balance that made him fall in love and linger outside her window hoping it would happen again—and *that's* why he saw the fire and ran in to save her.

David did not run after me. He'd never do anything in public that would look as if he was unreasonable. That would make obvious to everyone *he* was a crazy bitch. It never would have entered his mind; his mind has a bouncer at the door. Not like mine, open as a Greyhound depot. The woman with her wig askew who introduces herself as Princess Maud of Fife and tells you about her daughter who looks *just like you, dear.* Welcome to the prayer-strewn pews of my brain, worn smooth by thirty years of homeless heroes sleeping on them. Welcome, Princess Maud. Welcome, Dr. Strangelove.

I shut my door and began the longest forty-eight hours of my life. There would be no television, no *Masterpiece Theatre* or *Six Feet Under.* For once on Friday night Dr. S. and Maud were silent, replaced by a sort of white light, not a peaceful light, more like a strobe or like when you get thirsty for orange juice at 3:00 A.M. and are stunned by the light when you open the refrigerator door.

Doors were opening everywhere, flashbulbs going off in my face as if someone were collecting evidence, but no one was there. Exhibit A: Alice opens the cabinet and stares at a Folgers can. Exhibit B: Alice walks in circles around her coffee table banging her shin on the corner, her left shin because she always walks counterclockwise. Exhibit C: Alice lies flat on her back on the floor facing the ceiling, waving her arms and legs, making an angel in the snow.

Flowchart

I kept thinking there was no way I could go back to work on Monday and face him. I tried to analyze why not, but I got nowhere. What did I have to fear when after all *nothing had changed*? My plan to neutralize Fran had temporarily been nipped in the bud by a bunch of tulips. So what?

Surely I could walk into the office and act as if nothing had happened. In every sense the world acknowledges as real, nothing *had* happened. In every sense I acknowledge as real, however, everything had changed. I know I don't always see things clearly. I know sometimes my mind is a mirror shattered into shards that cut me even as they *are* me. But on this one question, I'm right. When the world denies anything has happened when the pink, breathing sky has become a gray slab, you want to make something happen they can't deny.

I'm not Joan of Arc but I understand her. It's always the strategy of the Inquisition to demand small compromises: to demand you admit 101 angels can dance on the point of a needle, but how can you when that would be to admit that angels are bodiless when they are anything but, and the fact that two angels cannot simultaneously occupy the same location because they have noses and skin and elbows and hair is crucial, the linchpin of existence?

I had to think it through, but how ridiculous. What does that even mean? In the whole history of humanity, has any important question ever been thought through? Did

Kennedy think through the Cuban Missile Crisis? Did Joseph and Mary think through the pros and cons of having a baby? Did my parents? I haven't thought anything through.

I did, however, get through the weekend without sleeping. I didn't climb the walls, but I thought of drawing on them. Maybe drawing a flowchart on my walls with a Magic Marker would help me think things through. In the end I decided that butcher paper would do. Either (a) David was telling the truth when he said he loved me, or (b) he was not. If he was telling the truth, either (a) he knows himself well enough that he was also being accurate, or (b) he does not and was not.

That may, however, assume a false premise. First it must be determined whether (a) human beings are capable of (1) knowing themselves and (2) loving, or (b) they (1) are not and (2) cannot. The available scientific research (a) is ambiguous on the question of whether human beings are capable of love, and (a1) the preponderance of the evidence suggests that even if they are capable, they are incapable of knowing in any particular instance if what they are engaged in is love or its opposite.

Ergo: David's statement that he loved me is either (a) meaningless and worthless, (b) worthless but meaningful, or (c) meaningless but precious, a diamond formed a hundred miles below the earth's surface and thrust up just far enough by a subterranean volcanic eruption to be found by a desperate miner (i.e., me).

Of course the other issue is that when someone says they love you, the *you* they love is only a sliver of who you are, and when they get to know more of you (a shard instead of a sliver), then (a) one or (b) both of you may realize either (x) the glimmering shard they love in fact crystallizes your essence, or (y) the shard they love is no more *you* than Fran's $600 sharkskin handbag is the essence of a two-ton fish whose 3,000 teeth are slick with the blood of turtles and tuna.

Aha, I've thought something through! Yes, I might have if only my heart were not beating faster as I remember him stating his meaningless proposition.

If David loved me, either (a) he would give me "space" to think things through, or no, not (a), never (a), the only answer is (b) he would call and ask if we could meet for coffee or he'd ring my doorbell or pound on my door until his knuckles bled and if I didn't answer he'd find a rock in the parking lot and if he couldn't he'd get a wrench from his car and if he didn't have one he'd get a book, a heavy one like *Swann's Way* or the Corolla owner's manual, or a can of tomato sauce from the corner grocery, and smash my kitchen window and cut himself crawling into my flat to tell me he just wanted to see if I was all right.

Yes, I'd call the police and have him arrested, but at least then I would know whether right now he is (a) lying in bed at midnight almost insanely hoping *I* will call *him*, or (b) fucking that sandy-haired cunt of a wife he left who I'd seen him with at the opera who looks like a diva of beach volleyball who'd as soon spike the ball down your throat—down mine—as dink it over the net. It would never occur to *her* to think anything through.

Stonehenge

How often during the past forty-eight hours have I almost called him? It would be the third time I've called him at this time of night over the past few months. Of course I never said a word when he answered, but you can tell a lot by the quality of the silence on the end of the line. I could tell he was alone, no one in the background asking who dared, or felt they had the right, to call that late.

I think it was unusual that he never sounded annoyed or impatient. He sounded open. You could say that calling David at 3:00 A.M. brought out the best in him. He didn't sound as if he'd say *Alice, what the hell are you doing?* if I identified myself. He sounded as if he'd put on his jeans and pick me up and take me to Mel's Drive-In, where no one drives in anymore but it's open twenty-four hours, and buy me coffee and not ask any questions.

It might be unrealistic to expect him not to ask any questions. I'd have to ask him not to ask, and that would be . . . out of the question, which is an interesting way to put it, worthy of Heidegger or one of those other Nazis. Whether or not to live as if nothing is out of the question *is* the question.

It must have been less than ten seconds of silence before he hung up, but it was a couple more than necessary, enough to give me a chance to change my mind and say something or just share a moment of silence as if we were at Point Reyes or the Vietnam Wall.

It's the stretching of silence a couple seconds beyond what's necessary, like during sex when you stop and are perfectly still for a couple seconds when stillness is the last thing you want but that is when the *other* thing comes in, not love, not pleasure or pain, something more like the light that falls on the winter solstice on the altar stone at Stonehenge.

More like the sound of a meteor shower, the silence of that golden swarm that would be deafening if you could hear it. As if your senses had changed their gender and you could smell what you see miles away, sage on the Marin headlands at the far side of the Bridge, hear the creak of the distant lighthouse as the beam turns, feel the rough wool of the fisherman's peacoat chafing his neck.

Sometimes I hear the voices of everything at once, all the silent things: the flagstones in the park, the dew on the pink thyme overgrowing their jagged edges; the stone Buddha, granite carved into the image of a man who after great struggle attained the stillness of stone; the burning tip of the cigarette dangling from the mouth of the ancient waitress taking her break on the sidewalk outside the dim sum parlor, having outlived three of her four children, savoring the last, sweet drag; the darkness of the night sky, the centuries of astronomers still unable to explain why it's dark when it's full of stars (they should ask me); the trigonometry of the angles formed by the lines between David's apartment and mine and our office in the Pyramid's shadow, the complex equations of tangents and sines and how they define the waves radiating from the iron grid of streetlamps.

And the infinite *what if's*: what if he'd had a different book the first time I saw him with *The Unbearable Lightness of Being*; what if on the Oregon coast that night I hadn't seen the fisherman with his hand on the blindfolded girl's shoulder as he guided her across the slick rocks; what if the high water had come a few minutes sooner and the moon jelly that washed ashore had been swept back out; what if the bus driver hadn't left us to dash into Connie's for coffee to-go and paused for a second on the sidewalk before coming back lost in his own *what if*; what if the electricity hadn't confined itself to the copper wire but leapt to the shallow pond on the porch slats after the rain; what if my mother hadn't been afraid to love me; what if my father had gone after the woman he wanted, the dancer, I'm sure it was a dancer or at least someone who liked to foxtrot at the Top of the Mark, someone who knew that way a dancer has of not exactly celebrating but *manifesting*; what if the earth were tilted one degree more on its axis than its 23-degree *obliquity*—I love that term, the obliquity of the ecliptic—whatever it is, it creates the seasons as we know them and an argument, a very good one, could be made that the seasons as we know them are not only what make life possible but what make it *worth the possibility*; what if there is a God and He or She or It loves beauty more than justice or bliss and knows there's more in Juliet's dagger than any happy ending (the sunset after the Crucifixion was unforgettable); what if a comet had not exploded 150 million years ago and a six-mile fragment not crashed into the Yucatán and raised a cloud of dust so vast that photosynthesis ceased on earth for long enough that the dinosaurs became extinct or evolved into birds (would we hear the same echoes now in the song of a nightingale?); what if the first man-slash-boy I kissed had not been such a jerk how could I let him hurt me like that I didn't even like his music I didn't like the white he'd painted his room it reminded me of Coast Guard uniforms I wanted to re-arrange his furniture I couldn't explain how it was turned the wrong way he thought I wanted to move in but it didn't have anything to do with that I literally couldn't sit on his couch unless he moved it against the north wall so the light and shadows would fall differently more sharply outlined but he wouldn't do it and by the next morning the whole school knew what a *crazy bitch* I was and I didn't even like his accent the way he pronounced my name as if it were one syllable *Alce* I let him slit me I let him *clean* me and I didn't even like his shoes.

Camera Obscura

What if I go into work tomorrow morning as if nothing has happened even though I haven't slept all weekend and look even more like a vamp than usual. What's the best-case scenario as I write this at the kitchen table with my Smith & Wesson still next to the pot of rose petal tea I made not to calm me down but to exult in the knowledge that nothing can ever calm me down again?

Should I wrap the revolver whose smooth grip I've come to love in newspaper and velvet and drop it down the garbage chute so it ends in the landfill in Little Hollywood, that neighborhood named for the legend that Mae West once kept a place in Frisco where she could rendezvous with her lover and not be shot by paparazzi? I like that as a resting place for my Lady Smith.

The worst-case scenario is I'm fired for insubordinate refusal of an Easter bouquet and on my way out the door with my shoebox of personal items David walks over my shadow with his new ballerina girlfriend. No, she would do modern dance. She'd be so fucking *interpretive* I'd vomit all over the sidewalk in the colors of Jackson Pollock's palette. But he didn't use a palette, did he? Fine, I'd do it his way: I'd let it spill straight from the paint can.

I always thought there was no way out of Vacaville for me, no way over the Tehachapis or through the Tunnel of Love. I've burned so many bridges *and* the ships that could have steamed under them out to sea. I've burned the wings of gannets and gulls so they ignite the night sky like flares from a scow. Scorched the headlands the bridges connect and when I look back all I see is a holy fire and what does that mean, *holy*, something you can't know because you can't look at it directly so you have to build one of those cameras and when the fire is in eclipse and your back is to it and the light passes through a pinhole (how much fire can pass through the eye of a needle?), you see an image of the eclipse on a plain white screen.

I still want to build that camera from a cardboard box to see the holy fire, and it might just be the one thing I can do.

Body Integrity Identity Disorder

I think I actually slept for a while, maybe half an hour. Isn't there a name for the condition that's the opposite of a phantom limb? Instead of sensing the presence of a limb you've lost, you're shocked each time you look in the mirror and you're all there.

One day I lost my sense of smell for a couple of hours, and even though somehow I still knew that Fran was wearing her Obsession and the Jade Palace was frying its onions, I also knew that everyone else was experiencing a dimension of aroma closed to me.

I know that others have had as awful a childhood as I did, if not worse, but they seem to have access to something I don't. Human beings can survive on little, the smell of bread as they pass a bakery, or smells we take for granted, the breath of oak trees, the wood of a park bench, or the sidewalk limestone, whose smell goes all the way back to the Pyramids when someone loved or feared someone enough to paint inside their tomb a blue heron in a marsh. The point is: some people can take in that psychic nourishment when they walk down Pine Street, and some people can't.

Sometimes I want to walk on crutches. I'd like to see the look on Fran's face and hear her *not say anything* if I went to work tomorrow on crutches. It doesn't take much to unnerve people. Forget the crutches: I could dye my hair blonde. I could still do that: I could go to the 24-hour Walgreens and get a bottle of Nice 'n Easy and go to work blonde. People would act as if I'd cut all my hair off with a dull scissors, and maybe I should do that, too. Maybe I should be myself. No, I'm already myself. What I mean is: maybe I should *look the part*.

Sometimes I feel as if I'm wearing iron shoes. Not iron—fucking tungsten. Every morning I need to find a new, unbelievable reason to get out of bed and drop a Pop-Tart in the toaster. There will be no revelation that pierces me with a diamond's glory and power, beautiful as a differential equation, no unknown variables brought into harmony or even relationship with an unknown function.

Let A for Alice equal the unknown function. Let David and Janette and Fran equal the unknown variables. My mistake was not to factor in the obvious fact that variables vary. I foolishly thought that just meant they might equal 16 or 17. I forgot it meant they could be a particle one minute and a wave the next, a meson one instant and decay in the next into a blue, spinning muon.

There are times (hours, nights) when whether light is a particle or a wave seems the most critical question in the world to me. There are times when light washes over me and simultaneously assaults me like a hot screed of needles.

What I'm thinking is there must be an alchemical process for turning particles into waves. What I'm thinking is maybe it's language, this cruel process of transmuting my pain into mine and Fran's and David's and Dr. Frost's and the FedEx man's, but maybe it's one form of cruelty I can forgive myself for.

Whatever it is, it's not lead into gold. It's lead into the bars of a cell or a stained-glass window where the reds and oranges of Nebuchadnezzar's furnace glow, lead into the glaze of a ruthless emperor's Tang Dynasty vase and the toxic white makeup on a geisha's face, lead into the aqueducts carrying water and death to Rome, lead into the organ pipes playing the dark chords of a fugue and into the paint that crazed artists from Caravaggio to Van Gogh, lead into the radiators distilling moonshine in the Blue Ridge of Georgia and the batteries that power car radios blaring Jay-Z or Pink, lead into the shields that guard cancer patients from gamma rays during XRT. Lead into bullets and buckshot and shrapnel and shells and dumdums and tracers and pipe bombs and land mines and cartridges and BBs and pellets and rounds and slugs and full metal jackets.

David's dream is to live in an unpainted wood home near the ocean (I never said he was original), but not too near because he doesn't want to take the view for granted. He says he wants to climb a hundred yards for it. Not a steep climb, just a rise, a hillside with mustard flowers where he can have a cigarette and look at God, as he puts it, which I take to mean look at something that quiets the voices in his mind—not silences them, just turns them down a notch.

Considering that I'm about the smartest person I know, I don't know why it took me so long to figure out I'm not the only one who hears them. It's not even unusual: it's the norm. *Typically* voices of hatred and ridicule. Yesterday I heard Mr. Warnick walking down the hall cursing the furnace, using a voice he must have heard somewhere, like the guy on a movie set who shouts *Action!* after the director has whispered it into his ear like a dirty joke. I won't give up my Lady Smith, but I've put it back in its box for a while, stashed it in the drawer with my cashmere where I won't see it all the time but I'll see it often enough not to take it for granted. For a walking chaos like me, maybe it's a good enough reason to live that I just want to see the looks on people's faces when I do.

Look: today is already tomorrow. It's been a long time since I've stayed awake long enough to see the sunrise. I'm not sure I ever have. I can't see the sun from my window, but I can see the way colors emerge over the rooftops from the gray so gradually, point by point, that you don't even notice the daylight. Sunrise is the one time you can see that light is both a particle and a wave.

I was in Pacifica once during a storm. The wind was so strong I couldn't walk to the end of the pier, just hold my ground leaning into it. All the fishermen had gone home, and the rain was a wall of water, a fist of a million cold kisses and stings that hit my face over and over. I wanted to stay there forever.

To think that ordinary light is like that too.

The Rock

I can see two landmarks out my window: Alcatraz and the Golden Gate Bridge. Alcatraz is the one that has always seemed hopeful to me. The bridge offers only two escape routes, down and across, and neither is hopeful. I've crossed it, and all I've found on the other side are redwood carvings of whales. *Across the bridge* is where people go to have their ashes scattered in the Pacific. There are so many ashes off the Mendocino coast the fish are suffocating. I prefer Alcatraz, which can be reached by no bridge.

I hadn't been born when the three men made their famous escape attempt. You'd think we'd know by now if they made it, but if they were smart enough to pull it off, they'd be patient enough to keep their mouths shut for the rest of their lives, maybe work a quiet job at a law firm as a word processor.

But this is what it took: they stole spoons from the prison mess and dug into the walls of their cells every night for years until there were openings just large enough to squeeze through to an abandoned maintenance hall. They soldered vacuum cleaner parts with silver from dimes to make a drill. And this is the part that's incredible: they had an accomplice play an accordion to disguise their noise.

How would you talk a man into playing an accordion in Cell Block A—someone who would never escape? He'd need to play it well enough that the guards and other prisoners wouldn't tell him to shut up, well enough that the entire prison from warden to dishwasher would stop what they're doing, not just entertained but rapt, listening to "Greensleeves," while three men in blue shirts got away.

They climbed up to the roof and down a drainpipe in the moonlight. They left dummy heads of soap and toilet paper and hair stolen from the prison barbershop floor in their beds. They set off into the bay on a raft they'd made of raincoats, and nobody knows if they even got as far as Angel Island.

At least that's the plan as it's been reconstructed from evidence after the fact. But it couldn't have been that simple. There must have been a thousand plans along the way that didn't pan out. How many close calls did they have before they came up with the accordion? That was an inspiration like God touching Adam's hand. They not only had to dig for hours to advance a fraction of an inch, they had to recalibrate constantly. They had to rethink. Every night for years, alone in their cells, they rethought it all.

That's pretty much what it takes, isn't it? It's not dunking a pan in the North Fork of the American River and coming up with a nugget of gold. It's cutting a jagged hole in concrete with a spoon and starving yourself so you can fit through. Patching together a raft of raincoats and glue, saying what the fuck. Waiting for the moon to go behind a cloud, then realizing you can't wait any longer and will have to risk it in the light.

Shoving off from shore, spitting out a prayer like a plug of chewing tobacco: What the fuck, you mothers. This broken, crazy bitch is going for broke. She's going to Angel Island on a raincoat. She's going to work.

Acknowledgments

I am truly grateful to the editors of the following publications, in which portions of this book first appeared (sometimes in different forms, sometimes in very different forms):

Gulf Coast: "Picnic";
Harvard Review: "Asylum" (as "Marine Biology");
Mid-American Review: "Songbird";
Mudlark: "Jury," "Rainforest," "Shadow Play," "Snowflakes," "The Wall";
Poetry: "Catchy Tunes," "The Gift."

It would be impossible to thank everyone whose insights contributed to this book, but I want especially to thank Robin Black, Diane Martin, Peg Alford Pursell, Melissa Stein, and Genanne Walsh for their remarkable and probing suggestions. The book would have been a dramatically different and weaker thing without their generosity. I also want to thank Tony Hoagland and Eleanor Wilner for their encouragement of this project at an early stage when it was hard to believe in it myself, the 13 Ways poetry group for their insights and patience with my fiction, and Peter Conners—BOA publisher, great editor, and fellow Deadhead—for his faith in the book, along with the whole BOA team: Melissa Hall, Jenna Fisher, cover designer Sandy Knight, and poet and typesetter Richard Foerster. Finally I want to thank Cheryl Morris, my wife, kick-ass attorney and kick-ass reader, for her apparently inexhaustible support and love.

About the Author

Robert Thomas is the author of *Door to Door* (2002, Fordham University Press), selected by Yusef Komunyakaa as winner of the Poets Out Loud Prize, and *Dragging the Lake* (2006, Carnegie Mellon University Press). He has received a poetry fellowship from the National Endowment for the Arts and won a Pushcart Prize. He lives with his wife in Oakland, California, and works as a legal secretary in San Francisco.

BOA Editions, Ltd. American Reader Series

No. 1 *Christmas at the Four Corners of the Earth*
Prose by Blaise Cendrars
Translated by Bertrand Mathieu

No. 2 *Pig Notes & Dumb Music: Prose on Poetry*
By William Heyen

No. 3 *After-Images: Autobiographical Sketches*
By W. D. Snodgrass

No. 4 *Walking Light: Memoirs and Essays on Poetry*
By Stephen Dunn

No. 5 *To Sound Like Yourself: Essays on Poetry*
By W. D. Snodgrass

No. 6 *You Alone Are Real to Me: Remembering Rainer Maria Rilke*
By Lou Andreas-Salomé

No. 7 *Breaking the Alabaster Jar: Conversations with Li-Young Lee*
Edited by Earl G. Ingersoll

No. 8 *I Carry A Hammer In My Pocket For Occasions Such As These*
By Anthony Tognazzini

No. 9 *Unlucky Lucky Days*
By Daniel Grandbois

No. 10 *Glass Grapes and Other Stories*
By Martha Ronk

No. 11 *Meat Eaters & Plant Eaters*
By Jessica Treat

No. 12 *On the Winding Stair*
By Joanna Howard

No. 13 *Cradle Book*
By Craig Morgan Teicher

No. 14 *In the Time of the Girls*
By Anne Germanacos

No. 15 *This New and Poisonous Air*
By Adam McOmber

No. 16 *To Assume a Pleasing Shape*
By Joseph Salvatore

No. 17 *The Innocent Party*
By Aimee Parkison

No. 18 *Passwords Primeval: 20 American Poets in Their Own Words*
Interviews by Tony Leuzzi

No. 19 *The Era of Not Quite*
By Douglas Watson

No. 20 *The Winged Seed: A Remembrance*
By Li-Young Lee

No. 21 *Jewelry Box: A Collection of Histories*
By Aurelie Sheehan

No. 22 *The Tao of Humiliation*
By Lee Upton

No. 23 *Bridge*
By Robert Thomas

Colophon

BOA Editions, Ltd., a not-for-profit publisher of poetry and other literary works, fosters readership and appreciation of contemporary literature. By identifying, cultivating, and publishing both new and established poets and selecting authors of unique literary talent, BOA brings high-quality literature to the public. Support for this effort comes from the sale of its publications, grant funding, and private donations.

The publication of this book is made possible, in part, by the special support of the following individuals:

Anonymous x 3
Armbruster Family Foundation
June C. Baker
Anne Germanacos
Suzanne Gouvernet
Michael Hall
X. J. & Dorothy M. Kennedy
Jack & Gail Langerak
Boo Poulin
Deborah Ronnen & Sherman Levey
Steven O. Russell & Phyllis Rifkin-Russell